THE ELUSIVE EARL

The Earl of Helstone, known as 'the Elusive Earl' because he will not be coerced into matrimony, is a patron of the turf. He arranges to stay at Epsom with Lady Chevington for the Derby of 1838, even though her daughter Calister warns him that if he accepts he will be tricked by her mother into marriage.

THE
ELUSIVE
EARL

The Elusive Earl

By

BARBARA CARTLAND

MAGNA PRINT BOOKS
Bolton-by-Bowland
Lancashire . England

British Library Cataloguing in Publication Data

Cartland, Barbara
    The elusive Earl. — Large print ed.
    I. Title
    823'.9'1F   PR6005.A765E/

    ISBN 0-86009-138-4

First Published in Great Britain by Hutchinson & Co
(Publishers) Ltd London 1976

Copyright © Barbara Cartland 1976

Published in Large Print 1978 by arrangement with
Hutchinson & Co (Publishers) Ltd London
USA Edition Bantam Books 1976

Printed and bound in Great Britain by
Redwood Burn Limited Trowbridge and Esher

Author's Note

The details of the English thoroughbreds are correct and are part of the history of Racing. The last horse to win the English Triple Crown (the 2,000 guineas, the Derby and the St. Leger) was Bahram in 1935. It is calculated that his pedigree contained among others 29,232 crosses of Godolphin Arabian, 44,079 of Darley Arabian and 64,032 of Byerley Turk. None of these three ever ran in a race.

There were only three Dictators of the Turf — Lord George Bentinck, the second, was succeeded by Admiral John Henry Rous, the most famous, and a supreme authority on handicapping.

The tale of Scham and Agba was eventually translated from the French by Colonel F. W. Alexander in 1867. The cat appears in portraits of Scham by Stubbs, Sartorious and Wootten.

Charles Green was one of the great pioneers of balloons. He made his first coal-gas ascent from Green Park in London during the celebrations of the Coronation of George IV. By 1835 he had made 200 flights and introduced the tail-rope.

In 1840 he planned a crossing of the Atlantic by balloon but this had to be abandoned when he was injured during a difficult balloon landing in Essex. After his 500th balloon ascent he retired and died in 1870.

1838

1

The horses thundered into the straight and the crowd on Newmarket Heath watching them uttered an audible sigh as they realized the favourite, wearing the blue and red colours of Lord Arkrie's stable, was in the lead.

Then a furlong later the gentlemen watching from the Jockey Club saw through their glasses another horse coming up on the outside.

He was moving easily and with an assurance that seemed to be lacking in the rest of the field who were now bunched together on the rails.

Steadily he drew up until at the last moment the crowd realized what was happening and there was a roar of appreciation.

For a moment the two horses were neck and neck; then the outsider, wearing orange with black crossed belts—colours well known in the racing world—passed the winning-post a length ahead.

Now there was no mistaking the cheer that rang out and Lord Arkrie turning from the front of the stand remarked sourly:

"Blast it, Helstone! I believe you are in league with the Devil himself! That was my race!"

The Earl of Helstone made no response to the outburst, but merely turned slowly to walk from the stand towards the unsaddling enclosure.

On the way he received congratulations from his friends, some sincere, some envious and a few sarcastic.

"Must you take all the prizes, Helstone?" one elderly Peer demanded in a disgruntled voice.

"Only the best of them," the Earl replied, and passed on to leave the Peer spluttering as he was unable to find a suitable retort.

He reached the enclosure just as his horse 'Delos' was led in amid the claps and cheers of the motley hordes which always frequented Newmarket Heath.

10

The Earl's jockey, a thin, cadaverous-looking young man who was seldom seen to smile, swung himself out of the saddle.

"Well done, Marson!" the Earl said, "your timing was excellent!"

"Thank you, M'Lord. I did exactly as Your Lordship told me."

"With excellent results!" the Earl said briefly.

He patted his horse and went from the unsaddling enclosure, not waiting for the results of the weighing-in.

As he walked back towards the Jockey Club he was joined by Lord Yaxley.

"That is a comfortable number of guineas in your pocket, Osric!" he remarked. "Not that you need them!"

"Did you back him?" the Earl enquired.

His friend hesitated for a moment.

"To be truthful, I hedged a little. Arkrie was so certain that his animal would come in first."

"He has been boasting about it for weeks," the Earl remarked.

"So you decided to show him up?" Lord Yaxley said with a smile. "Well, you have certainly been successful! I believe he staked three thousand guineas on the race. He will be a bitter enemy from now on."

"That will be nothing new!" the Earl replied.

They reached the Jockey-Stand and went to the Bar at the back.

"May I offer you a drink?" the Earl enquired.

"I think it is the least you can do, Osric," Lord Yaxley replied. "Dammit all, money always goes to money! That is what my old father always used to say."

"You should trust your friends," Lord Helstone said coldly. "I told you that Delos was a good horse."

"The trouble is that you did not say it positively enough!" Lord Yaxley complained. "Arkrie was shouting the merits of his beast from the house-tops."

Lord Helstone said nothing but merely accepted the glass of champagne that had been poured out for him.

Lord Yaxley raised his glass.

"Your health, Osric!" he said, "and may you, as you always do, go on succeeding in everything you undertake!"

"You flatter me," the Earl remarked dryly.

"On the contrary," Lord Yaxley contradicted, "you are abominably, infuriatingly and invariably first past the post, and not only on the race-course!"

He gave his friend a sly glance as he spoke then he said with an irritated note in his voice:

"Curse it, Osric, but you might look a little more elated! After all, you have just won one of the best races of the Season and shown once again your thoroughbreds are superior to anyone else's. You ought to be jumping for joy!"

"I am too old, my dear fellow, for such youthful exuberance," the Earl answered. "Besides, although it is extremely satisfactory to prove that my horses are superior, with my trainer and jockey prepared to do what I tell them, I see no reason for any extravagant elation."

Lord Yaxley put his glass down with a bang.

"You exasperate me, Osric," he said. "There are times when I miss the man you were in your youth, when we were wild and irreverent and everything seemed amusing and an adventure. What has happened?"

"As I have just told you, we have grown older," the Earl remarked.

"I do not believe it is age," Lord Yaxley said. "I think it is just being satiated; over-stuffed with the good things of life; like attending one of those dinners that used to be given at Carlton House in my father's day!"

He drank some more champagne before he went on:

"He has so often talked of how there would be thirty-five *entrées* and the Regent ate so much he could hardly rise from his chair at the end of a meal!"

"I may have many faults," the Earl said, "but I do not overeat."

"No, but you indulge yourself in other ways," Lord Yaxley said shrewdly.

Someone came up at that moment to congratulate the Earl on his win and there was no chance of further conversation.

But later on that evening in his host's elegant house on the outskirts of the town Lord Yaxley returned to the assault.

"I suppose you know, Osric," he said, "that you will have offended a large number of your friends by leaving the dinner given in your honour so early?"

14

"I doubt if anyone has noticed our departure," the Earl replied. "They were, all of them, too foxed to count heads!"

"And you, of course, are excessively sober!" Lord Yaxley remarked.

He threw himself down in a comfortable leather armchair in front of the log-fire which was burning brightly.

"If there is one thing I really dislike," the Earl said, "it is drinking myself under the table and being, in consequence, unable to watch the morning gallops."

"You sound sanctimonious!"

"I thought you were complaining that I indulged myself too often," the Earl said with a twist of his lips.

"Not where food and drink is concerned," Lord Yaxley said, "but in other ways."

"Then if it is not wine it must be 'women and song!' although I cannot imagine why you take it upon yourself to give me a lecture."

"It is because I am fond of you," Lord Yaxley answered, "and because we have been friends for such a long time. I hate to see you growing more bored and more indifferent year by year."

15

"Who said I was bored?" the Earl enquired sharply.

"It is obvious," Lord Yaxley replied. "I was watching your face on the course today. There was not even a glint of satisfaction in your eyes as Delos beat Arkrie's horse. That is unnatural, Osric, as you well know."

The Earl did not reply but merely lay back in his deep armchair looking at the flames.

"What is the matter?" Lord Yaxley asked in a different tone of voice, "is it Genevieve?"

"Perhaps!"

"Do you intend to marry her?"

"Why should I?"

"Unlike Arkrie, she is proclaiming her love for you to all and sundry."

"I cannot prevent her from making a fool of herself," the Earl said, "but I assure you it is not based on any encouragement from me."

"She would look well at the head of your table and undoubtedly ravishing in the Helstone diamonds."

The Earl said nothing for a moment, then he said slowly:

"I have no wish to marry Genevieve."

Lord Yaxley gave a little sigh.

"Quite frankly, Osric, I am glad. I was not certain if your heart was involved or not, but Genevieve would doubtless bore you in time just as much as every other Charmer you have discarded one by one."

He gave a short laugh and added:

"Have you ever noticed how she always sits so that you are looking at her profile? She told me once that someone — I have forgotten who — had said to her that if Frances Stewart had not been the model for Britannia they would have chosen her."

"Frances Stewart, if my history is correct," the Earl said with a sarcastic note in his voice, "refused her favours to Charles II, which was why he remained infatuated with her until her face was disfigured by smallpox."

Lord Yaxley laughed again.

"No-one can accuse Genevieve of refusing you."

The Earl did not reply and after a moment Lord Yaxley continued:

"But then you never are refused, are you, Osric? I am beginning to think that

that is the trouble."

"What trouble?" the Earl enquired.

"It could account for your boredom. Now I think about it, it must in time become tedious to know you are always going to turn up the winning card, always bring down the bird you aim at, always be in at the kill."

"More flattery!"

"All the same, I am speaking the truth, and you know it!" Lord Yaxley said, "and the truth is—you are bored, Osric!"

"Then what do you suggest I do about it?" the Earl enquired.

"I wish I could answer that question. There must be some prize you covet somewhere; some mountain you have not climbed; some battle you have not won."

"Perhaps a war would be a solution!" the Earl remarked. "At least then one would be dealing with the fundamental effort of staying alive."

"You know I am not certain," Lord Yaxley said as if he were following his own train of thought, "that it would not be best for you to get married! It might induce you to spend more time in the country; for I do realize that huge mansion of yours filled with the portraits of your ancestors would be excessively gloomy if you lived in it by yourself."

"You think marriage would be a solution?"

"Not for Genevieve — she would not settle down anywhere!" Lord Yaxley said quickly. "But there must be a woman somewhere who would take your fancy and would not bore you to tears."

"There are quite a number."

"I am not talking about love-affairs, you idiot!" Lord Yaxley exclaimed. "I am talking about marriage to some nice, respectable young woman who will give you children, especially a son. That at least would be an interest you have not tried so far."

"But to get a son I would have to suffer the banal conversation, the half-witted meanderings of the respectable young girl," the Earl said. "I assure you, Yaxley, Genevieve would be preferable to that!"

"I must admit, I looked over this Season's débutantes at a Ball last week," Lord Yaxley said. "I had to put in an appearance, because it was being given for one of my nieces. I have never seen a more depressing sight!"

"That is the answer to your suggestion."

"A débutante would be too young for you, that I agree," Lord Yaxley conceded. "We will both be thirty next year, and that is far too old for Nursery games."

"And what is the alternative?" the Earl enquired.

"There must be a sophisticated, charming, intelligent widow about somewhere," Lord Yaxley remarked.

"So we are back to Genevieve again!"

There was silence between the two men as they were both thinking of the alluring, irrepressible and at times outrageous Lady Genevieve Rodney.

She had been widowed two years previously, and the moment she was out of mourning she had set the social world by the ears by the manner in which she defied convention.

But the gentlemen found her irresistible and her small house in Mayfair was besieged day and night by her innumerable admirers.

It was not surprising that she set her cap at the Earl of Helstone.

He was not only one of the richest men

in England, but he was, in many women's opinion, by far the best-looking.

It was however with reason that he was nicknamed 'The Elusive Earl'.

Ever since he had left school he had been pursued by ambitious mothers and by women who found both his handsome face and his well-filled pockets irresistible.

But he had eluded every effort to lure him into the matrimonial net and was extremely fastidious in selecting the recipients of his affections.

It had however amused him, when Lady Genevieve was the toast of St. James's and pursued by every Buck and Beau of the social world, to sweep her off from under their very noses.

She had made no pretence that he was the first man to capture her heart. Nor was he the first lover she had taken after her husband's death.

But during the months they had been together she had made it very clear that she intended that he should be the last.

Lady Genevieve's heart was a vacillating organ and the Earl was never quite certain how much her protestations of true love rested on the fact that he could provide for her as lavishly as she desired, and give her a position in society that would be un-equalled by anyone outside the Royal family.

The Helstones in fact had Royal blood in their veins, and it was known that their genealogical family tree with all its quar-terings was a headache to the College of Heralds.

Apart from that, the Earl had achieved on his own merits a position of importance in the House of Lords which made him a person to be reckoned with and his opinion to be sought.

And no-one would deny that he reigned supreme in the sporting world.

He had concentrated on breeding thoroughbreds and had actually imported Arab stallions, as the earlier breeders had done, to improve his own strain.

Delos, however, the horse which had won the race at Newmarket was a direct descendant of the famous Eclipse which had sired so many great racehorses and whose successes were still spoken of with bated breath in racing circles.

Eclipse had been named after the great eclipse that occurred in 1764, the year of his birth, and had been bred by William, Duke of Cumberland, who died however a year later.

The horse was then bought at the Duke's disposal sale by Mr. William Wildeman, a Smithfield meat salesman for seventy-five guineas.

Eclipse made his first appearance on a racecourse in the 'Noblemen and Gentlemen's Plate' at Epsom in 1769. His breathtaking performance made everyone with a knowledge of horseflesh realize that here was a phenomenon that would stand out for all time in the history of racing.

The Earl of Helstone as a boy had heard his father talk of Eclipse and of his win being recorded by the famous words 'Eclipse first, the rest nowhere'.

He had a feeling that Delos, or one of the other horses in his stable, might prove to be what he sought.

But one could never be sure until the animal had run in a number of the great races on the flat.

"Perhaps to own an 'Eclipse' or a horse to equal him," the Earl told himself now, "would be the most satisfactory ambition a man could ask of life."

He looked up at a picture over the mantelpiece. It was a portrait of Eclipse painted by George Stubbs.

The dark chestnut colour of the horse was set off by a white blaze and white stocking on his off hind-leg. He was a big horse by the standard of his time, standing 15 hands 3 inches.

He had a great length from hip to hock, a short and powerful forearm and long sloping shoulders.

These qualities had given him his tremendous stride, which combined with a fiery, aggressive temperament, won for him an indelible place in the annals of the Turf.

Lord Yaxley followed his friend's eyes and said:

"I grant you Delos made a spectacular finish today. Do you think he can win the Derby?"

"I have not yet made up my mind if I will enter him," the Earl replied.

"You will be pressed to do so," Lord Yaxley said.

"I assure you I shall follow my own judgement in the matter," the Earl

answered. "Nobody yet has been successful in pressing me to do anything I did not
wish to do."

His friend looking at him across the
hearth decided this was true.

He knew better than anyone else how
determined and unyielding the Earl could
be once he had made up his mind.

He was extremely fond of him, and they
had been friends ever since they had been
children in their perambulators.

They had been to the same school,
served in the same Regiment, and strangely enough they had inherited their titles
in the same year.

But while the Earl was immeasurably
richer and more important on a social
scale than Lord Yaxley, the latter was
comfortably off, and there were few important families in Great Britain who
would not have welcomed him as a son-in-
law.

"To win the Derby which I do not think
could be achieved by any other horse,
would be a satisfaction," Lord Yaxley
said.

"I agree with you," the Earl remarked.
"But if I do not enter Delos, there is

always Zeus or Pericles."

"The trouble is you have too many plums in the pudding!" Lord Yaxley smiled.

"Still gunning for me, Willoughby?"

The Earl rose to his feet to walk across the comfortably furnished room.

"And after the Derby, I suppose I try for the Gold Cup at Ascot, and after Ascot the St. Leger?"

"Why not?" Lord Yaxley enquired.

"The same old round," the Earl remarked. "You are right, Willoughby, I am beginning to find it a dead bore. I think I will go abroad."

"Abroad?" Lord Yaxley ejaculated, sitting up in his chair. "What on earth for? And surely not during the Season?"

"I think it is the Season I find so extremely dull," the Earl remarked. "Those endless Balls and parties. The invitations pouring in. The chatter, the gossip and the scandal! I have done it so many times before. My God! It is a headache!"

"You are spoilt, Osric, just spoilt!" Lord Yaxley exclaimed. "Why, there is not a man in the whole country who would not give his right arm to be standing in your shoes!"

"I wish I could think of something for which I was prepared to sacrifice my right arm," the Earl replied.

Lord Yaxley was silent for a moment, his eyes on his friend's face. Then he asked quietly:

"Something in particular is making you blue devilled?"

The Earl did not reply but sat in front of the fireplace looking into the flames.

"It is Genevieve, is it not?" Lord Yaxley said after a moment.

"Partly," the Earl admitted.

"What can she have done?"

"As a matter of fact, if you want to know the truth," the Earl said, "she tells me she is having a baby!"

Lord Yaxley looked at him in astonishment, then he said sharply:

"It is not true!"

The Earl turned from his contemplation of the fire to look at his friend.

"What do you mean by that?"

"I mean what I say," Lord Yaxley answered. "It is a lie, because Genevieve told my youngest sister a long time ago that, owing to a fall out hunting when she was a girl, the Doctors have said it is impossible for her to bear a child!"

He paused, then he added:

"That was one of the reasons why I was so afraid you might marry her. It is not my business, of course, and I did not want to interfere, but I would have told you before you took her up the aisle."

The Earl sat back again in the arm-chair.

"Are you sure of this, Willoughby?"

"Dead certain," Lord Yaxley replied. "My sister who was at the same school as Genevieve, told me about the accident at the time. When she married Rodney he was longing for her to give him a son. According to my sister they consulted half-a-dozen Doctors, but there was nothing that could be done about it."

There was silence for a moment, then he said:

"If you ask me, Genevieve is determined to get you by hook or by crook, and the whole story is a concoction in the hope that you will behave like a gentleman."

The Earl rose to his feet.

"Thank you, Willoughby! You have

28

indeed taken a load off my mind! And now I think we should retire to bed. If we are going to watch the gallops we must leave the house at six o'clock."

"Well, all I can say is I am thankful that I did not drink deep!" Lord Yaxley remarked as they walked towards the door.

He knew that the Earl had no desire to discuss further the subject of Lady Geneveive.

At the same time Lord Yaxley was glad that the Earl had raised the subject first and he had been able to give him without embarrassment the information that had been hovering on his lips for a long time.

Close though they were, Lord Yaxley was aware that the Earl could be extremely reserved where his love-affairs were concerned, and he knew as they walked up the stairs towards their bedrooms that only in the most exceptional circumstances would he have admitted, as he had to-night, what was troubling him.

"Blast Genevieve!" Lord Yaxley said to himself as they parted on the landing and went to their respective bedrooms.

He was quite certain that it was the

thought of being forced to marry the delectable widow that had spoiled the Earl's enjoyment of winning the race this afternoon and made him more than usually remote and difficult.

But with or without the problem of Genevieve, Lord Yaxley had been aware for some time that the Earl was bored with the social round and his own proverbial luck which made everything he touched turn to gold.

"Osric is right!" he told himself as he got into bed. "What he needs is a war or a similar challenge to give him an incentive."

It was all the fault of having too much money, Lord Yaxley decided.

The Earl was so unbelievably rich that there was really nothing he could not buy.

Horses, women, possessions — they all required little effort on his part.

Perhaps it was a surfeit of success which had made the Earl grow cynical, and even to his best friends there was now a hardness about him that was increasingly perceptible.

It showed in his face.

It was almost impossible to imagine

that a man could be more handsome, but even when there was a glint of amusement in his eyes, those who knew him well seldom found there was anything soft or gentle about his expression.

He expected perfection in the performance of duty by his servants and his employees, and it was seldom he was disappointed.

His houses and his Estates were admirably administered and, if there were minor difficulties and problems, they were not brought to his notice.

He employed the best Agents, Managers, Secretaries and Attorneys. He was the Commander-in-Chief, who planned a campaign and was seldom, if ever, disappointed in the results.

"He has too much!" Lord Yaxley said to himself before he fell asleep, wondering what could be the solution.

After the next day's racing the two noblemen drove back together to London, the Earl tooling his Phaeton drawn by a team of superlative horses and covering the mileage in what was, they were certain, record time.

As they reached Helstone House in

Piccadilly, Lord Yaxley said:

"Am I meeting you at dinner tonight? I believe we have both been invited by the Devonshires."

"Have we?" the Earl asked indifferently. "My secretary will have a list of my engagements."

"And that reminds me," Lord Yaxley said. "Are you going to stay with Lady Chevington again for the Derby? I am sure she has asked you."

"I believe I did receive an invitation from her," the Earl replied.

"Do you intend to accept?"

There was a moment's pause. Then as the Earl drew his horses to a standstill outside the front door, he answered:

"Why not? It is far the most comfortable house near Epsom, and at least her parties are sometimes amusing."

"Then we can go together," Lord Yaxley said. "Will you drive me down, Osric—unless you have other plans?"

"I shall be delighted to give you a lift."

The two men parted, Lord Yaxley being driven by the Earl's groom to his lodgings which were only two streets away.

The Earl walked across the Hall and

into the Library.

He was there only for a moment before his secretary, Mr. Grotham, came into the room and bowed.

"Anything important, Grotham?" the Earl enquired.

"A great number of invitations, My Lord, but I will not trouble you with them now, and several private letters. I have put them on your desk."

The Earl walked to the desk and saw four envelopes written in what was obviously female handwriting.

Mr. Grotham was always too tactful to open any letter or note which he thought might be personal, and after years of service with His Lordship he was extremely astute in recognizing a woman's hand.

The Earl saw now that three of the letters were from Lady Genevieve. There was no mistaking her dashing, over-elaborate style, and as he looked down at them, his lips tightened.

He had not referred again to the matter which Lord Yaxley and he had discussed last night, but the anger that the information had aroused still seethed within him.

How dare she attempt, he asked himself, to catch him by the oldest trick in the world, and how could he have been such a fool as to credit for one moment that she was telling him the truth?

When he had started his love-affair with Lady Genevieve he had no intention of it becoming serious. He had expected it to be a light-hearted liaison between two sophisticated people who understood the rules of the game.

That Genevieve had fallen in love with him, according to what she told him, had not perturbed him in the slightest, except for the fact that she seemed determined to proclaim her affection for him noisily and incessantly.

He had found her desirable, extremely fascinating and one of the most passionate women he had ever known in his life.

She amused him and he had paid for her favours with diamonds, rubies and a stream of exorbitant bills from Bond Street dressmakers. He had also provided her with a carriage and horses that were the envy of all her friends.

Never for one moment had the Earl considered marrying Genevieve Rodney.

She was the type of woman who, he knew from past experience, was incapable of being faithful either to a husband or to a lover.

He was quite certain that, should the temptation arise, she would not hesitate to deceive him behind his back by taking to her bed any man who aroused her desires.

But what he did not realize was that Genevieve found him irresistible, simply and solely because, as had been said so often about him, he was elusive.

There was something about the Earl which no woman had ever been able to capture.

Even in the closest moments of intimacy she always knew that she did not possess him, that he was not completely and whole-heartedly hers. So because the Earl eluded Genevieve, she, being perhaps for the first time in her life the seeker, not the sought, fell in love!

She did not possess a deep nature and her emotions were very much on the surface, but she was a fiery creature with an insatiable craving for any man who took her fancy.

With the Earl she found her heart was unsatisfied, however competent a lover he proved in every other way.

She wanted him at her feet. She wanted him subservient as other men had been. She wanted to capture him, and because he eluded her, she made up her mind to marry him.

Besides any personal desire in the matter the Earl was a *parti* to whom no female in the length and breadth of the country was likely to say no.

Apart from the tales of his vast fortune, his estates and his priceless possessions, a woman had only to look at him, tall, broad-shouldered, handsome and confidently sure of himself, to feel her heart turn over in her breast.

Genevieve exerted every wile in her extensive repertoire to enthrall the Earl.

She found it easy to arouse his desires and he was extremely generous. But he never professed to love her: there was always a fairly cynical twist to his lips and a slightly mocking note in his voice when he talked to her.

She knew only too well that she was not essential to him. She was never quite certain when he left her when she would see him again. She was not even sure that he missed her when he was away from her.

In fact he drove her crazy!

"When are you going to marry me, Osric?" she asked daringly one night as she lay close in his arms and the flames of the fire gave the only light in her flower-scented bedroom.

"You are greedy, Genevieve," the Earl replied.

"Greedy?" she questioned.

"Yes," he answered. "I gave you a diamond necklace yesterday. Last week it was rubies, and I think the week before that it was an emerald brooch which took your fancy — and now you want more!"

"Only a small gold ring!" she whispered.

"That is the one thing I cannot afford."

"But why? We would be happy together — you know we would."

"What do you call happiness?" the Earl questioned evasively.

"Being with you," Genevieve replied. "You know that I make you happy."

She moved nearer to him and threw

back her head so that her lips invited his.

He looked down at her and she could not read the expression in his eyes.

"I love you!" she said. "Marry me — please, marry me!"

In answer he had kissed her passionately and the fire which, in both of them, was never far from the surface, burst into a blaze.

They were consumed by the heat of it and it was only later when she was alone that Genevieve remembered he had not answered her question.

Now the Earl was angry and his eyes were hard as he looked down at the three letters on which his name was inscribed with the same imperious flourish.

Deliberately he reached for another letter which was in a writing he did not recognize.

"If you do not need me, My Lord, and have no further instructions," Mr. Grotham said respectfully, "may I retire?"

"I believe I am dining at the Devonshire's tonight?" the Earl asked.

"Yes, My Lord. I have ordered your carriage."

"What answer did you make to Lady Chevington's ivitation to Epsom?"

"You said you would think about it on your return, My Lord."

"Accept!" the Earl said briefly.

"Very good, My Lord, and may I congratulate Your Lordship on your win today?"

"The grooms told you, I suppose?" the Earl said. "It was very satisfying. I think Delos will prove to be a great horse."

"I hope so, My Lord. I hope so indeed!"

"Did you have a few shillings on him?" the Earl asked.

"Yes, My Lord, as did all the household. We all have great faith in Your Lordship's judgement."

"Thank you!"

Mr. Grotham left the room closing the door quietly behind him.

The Earl realized he was holding a letter in his hand and slit it open. He read it and then stood staring at it in surprise.

Written in a very elegant and neat hand, in the centre of a plain sheet of paper, were the words:

"If Your Lordship would hear something very much to your advantage, will you be on the South side of the bridge over the Serpentine at nine o'clock tomorrow, Friday morning? It is of the utmost import!"

"What the devil does this mean?" the Earl asked himself.

There was no signature and he thought perhaps it was a hoax.

He had in the past often received letters from women he did not know, but they had always signed their names and been very careful to ensure that their addresses were on the writing-paper so that he could get in touch with them.

But there was nothing with this note except for the bald message.

He thought that it might perhaps be a method of publicizing a new night-haunt; but that was unlikely seeing that there was no address. The same applied to a letter which might have come from one of the pretty Cyprians who were always on the lookout for new clients.

The Earl had on several occasions been invited to parties by women he did not know. These had turned out to be either orgies or an assignation with some fair

40

charmer who expected to be heavily reimbursed for her favours.

This letter could be neither of these things, and perhaps, the Earl thought, it was in fact exactly what it purported to be — a message inviting him to a rendezvous where he might learn something to his advantage! Although what that could be he had no idea!

There was no doubt that the handwriting was educated and the writing-paper expensive.

He rang the bell which stood on his desk and instantly the door was opened by a flunkey.

"Send Barker to me!" the Earl ordered.

A few seconds later his Butler came into the room.

"You wanted me, M'Lord?"

"Yes, Barker. Can you remember who brought this note?" He held out the envelope as he spoke.

"Yes, M'Lord," the Butler replied. "I was in the Hall, as a note had just been delivered for Your Lordship by a groom wearing the livery of Lady Genevieve Rodney."

"And this one. . ." the Earl enquired.

". . . was brought to the door by a ragged boy, M'Lord. I was in fact surprised that the letter looked as it did, seeing who delivered it!"

"Did you ask him where he came from?" the Earl enquired.

He knew that Barker was extremely inquisitive, and that little went on in the household of which he was not aware.

"As it happened, M'Lord," Barker replied with dignity, "I thought it wise to ask the boy some questions."

"What did he tell you?" the Earl asked.

"He informed me, M'Lord, that a lady had given him 6d to bring the letter to this house. He's a boy who hangs about the Square, M'Lord, hoping for a chance of holding a horse or running a message."

"So that is all he told you?"

"That's all, M'Lord."

The Earl told himself as he put the note down that it would be ridiculous to put himself out to meet some unknown person who wrote in such a manner, and that if he did so he would undoubtedly find that it was a new method of touching him for a small loan.

Then as he rose from his desk, leaving

Lady Genevieve's notes unopened, he knew that however much he might jeer at himself for being so curious, he would undoubtedly be on the south side of the Serpentine bridge tomorrow morning at nine o'clock!

. . .

The Earl went to bed later than he had intended, because he had become involved in a political argument at Devonshire House which went on into the early hours of the morning.

He was therefore somewhat disagreeable when he was woken from a deep sleep by his valet, at his usual hour of eight o'clock.

His bath was prepared for him on the hearth-rug in his bedroom in front of the fire. Because he disliked the water getting cold the Earl resisted an inclination to lie back against his pillows, and rose from his bed.

Twenty minutes later he descended to the Breakfast-Room to look with a jaundiced eye at the long row of silver dishes laid out on a side-table.

He inspected them and telling Barker to help him to kidneys cooked in cream he sat down at the breakfast table.

When the kidneys came he waved them away and asked for a plain lamb chop.

When he had eaten he began to feel better and told himself that the reason he was not feeling in his usual good health was the fact that the rooms at Devonshire House had been over-heated, and that the brandy supplied by the Duke had been of inferior quality.

As he had told Lord Yaxley, he seldom drank to excess and, while he had not been in the slightest degree drunk last night, he had however sipped brandy while they were talking until it was nearly dawn.

He therefore found it difficult to sleep when he eventually reached his bed and that, combined with the long drive back from Newmarket, had made him unusually fatigued.

He decided that what he needed was fresh air and went out of the front door to find a black stallion which he had bought only the previous week at Tattersall's was awaiting him.

Suddenly the Earl found that both his headache and his disagreeableness had dispersed in the spring sunshine.

The horse was magnificent! There was no doubt about that!

His muscles were rippling under his shiny black coat, while he tossed his head and pranced about in a manner which told the Earl that he was an animal worth breaking in to his touch.

Two grooms were striving to hold the stallion steady and finding it almost impossible to keep their hold on him as the Earl swung himself into the saddle.

As the animal bucked and reared to show his independence, it took the Earl a little while to get him under control.

They set off down Piccadilly and had reached Hyde Park before the Earl knew with a sense of triumph that once again he was the master!

There was nothing the Earl enjoyed more than a battle with a horse who was determined not to be subservient to his will.

They had a number of tussles before finally the Earl, pressing his tall hat firmly down upon his head, took the stallion at a sharp pace down the Row.

Away from the fashionable part where it was considered socially incorrect to gallop, the Earl gave the horse his head and galloped him hard over the grass until there was a glimmer of silver ahead and he realized they were nearing the Serpentine.

Pulling his mount to a trot he took his gold watch from his vest-pocket and looked at the time.

It was in fact just on nine o'clock!

He had intended not to be punctual — it never hurt to keep someone as importunate as the writer of the note waiting — but owing to the speed at which he had galloped he was in fact on time.

Steadily he rode towards the bridge and saw as he drew near to it that there was nobody there.

"It must have been a hoax!" the Earl told himself.

Nevertheless because he was curious to know why anyone should take the trouble to play such a trick on him, he pulled the stallion to a standstill and stood looking at the long silver stretch of water.

The horse fidgeted a little, and the

Earl had just made up his mind to leave and continue with his ride when he saw coming towards him through the trees a woman riding at a pace which almost equalled his own a little earlier.

She was wearing a green riding-habit and the veil which encircled her hat flew out behind her like a flag.

He stood waiting as she drew nearer and he noticed with an experienced eye that she was riding an extremely well-bred animal.

Then to his astonishment, as the horse came nearer still, seeming to gallop straight at him, the woman threw herself from the saddle to fall to the ground directly in front of him.

The Earl was so surprised that for a moment he could only stare at her. Then hastily, as she appeared to be lying still, he dismounted, tied his stallion's reins with an expert hand to a post on the side of the bridge and went to her side.

As he reached her he saw that her eyes were closed, but as he bent down and put out his hands, she opened them.

"Are you the Earl of Helstone?" she asked.

47

"Yes," he answered. "Are you all right?"

"Of course I am all right!" she answered in a surprisingly firm tone. "But I have something to tell you and we shall have to be quick about it!"

"What is it?" the Earl asked.

She had obviously suffered no damage and was in no pain, but she continued to lie on the ground, although now she supported herself on one elbow and her head was raised.

She was surprisingly attractive, he thought, with fair hair with a touch of red in it showing under the brim of her dark hat, a very white skin, and large grey-green eyes that seemed almost to fill her small face.

She was young, the Earl realized, and yet her voice had a decisive note in it which he did not associate with a young girl.

"You have been asked," she said, "to stay with Lady Chevington for the Epsom races?"

"I have," the Earl answered.

"You must refuse! Write and make any excuse you like, but on no account accept the invitation!"

"But why?" the Earl asked in bewilderment. "And why should it concern you?"

The girl was just about to answer him, when there was the sound of thudding hoofs and a groom came hurrying towards them.

He was a middle-aged man and when he saw his mistress lying on the ground he exclaimed in consternation:

"What's happened to you, Miss Calista? Have you hurt yourself?"

"No, I am all right, Jenkins," the girl replied. "Go and catch Centaur."

"Now, Miss Calista, you knows I won't be able to do that. . ." the man began.

The Earl looked up at him sharply.

"You heard what the lady said. Catch her horse and bring it here!"

The groom recognized the voice of authority and touched his cap.

"Very good, Sir."

He spurred the horse he was riding and moved away.

The girl raised herself until she was in a sitting position. Then to the Earl's astonishment she puckered her lips together and emitted a long, low whistle, followed by a shorter one.

The horse she had been riding immediately raised his head from where, a little way to the left of them, he was placidly eating the grass.

The groom had nearly reached him, but at his approach the horse turned away, trotting away for a dozen yards to put down his head again. The groom followed him only for the same thing to happen.

The Earl looked down at the girl beside him.

"You taught him to behave like that?" he said. "And he did not throw you — you threw yourself off!"

"Of course Centaur would never throw me!" the girl answered, "but I wanted to talk to you, and if Jenkins thought we had met by arrangement he would have told Mama."

"Who is your mother?" The Earl enquired.

"Lady Chevington!"

He looked at her in perplexity.

"Then why are you telling me I am not to accept your mother's invitation to Epsom?"

"Because," the girl answered, "if you come to stay, she will make you marry me!"

For a moment the Earl thought she must be joking, but as he looked into her eyes he realized there was a serious expression in them and there was no doubt that she meant what she said.

There was a faint smile on his lips as he said:

"I assure you that I can look after myself. If I do stay in your house for the races, I will make no offer for your hand, if that is what is worrying you!"

"Do not be so ridiculous!" Calista replied sharply. "You do not understand what I am trying to say. You will not have the chance of offering for me, nor I of refusing you, which I assure you I should! You will be forced to marry me. You will be tricked into it and there will be no honourable escape."

The Earl rose to his feet.

"I am sure you mean well in trying to warn me," he said, "but I do not quite understand why you should be so perturbed. I promise you, Miss Calista, I have no intention of marrying anyone!"

"And I have no intention of marrying you!" she replied almost rudely. "But if you disregard my warning and accept Mama's invitation, she will contrive that we shall be married."

The Earl laughed.

"I cannot imagine any circumstances in which I could be coerced into accepting a situation which is not of my making," he said. "You may rest assured, Miss Calista, that what you fear will not happen."

Calista rose to her feet.

"You are a fool!" she said. "I might have realized I was wasting my time in writing to you!"

She shook the dust from her riding-habit and added:

"Why do you think the Duke of Frampton married my elder sister Ambrosine, or the Marquis of Northaw my second sister Beryl?"

She waited as if she expected the Earl to reply, but as he said nothing and only looked at her speculatively she said:

"They found themselves engaged to be married because Mama had made up her mind to have them as sons-in-law. Now she has chosen you as . . . my husband!"

"The idea obviously fills you with horror!" the Earl said, a sarcastic note in his voice.

"I imagined you would have more sense than to treat it as a joke! You are spoken of as being intelligent," she said, "but I was obviously misled. All right, come to Chevington Court, but I swear I will not marry you, whatever happens!"

"What could happen?" the Earl enquired.

"You will see!" she replied ominously, "and let me tell you that Mama will win a bet of one thousand guineas the day our engagement is announced in the *Gazette*!"

"I assure you she will be a loser," the Earl said.

He thought Calista gave him a contemptuous glance before she looked to where the groom was still vainly trying to catch her horse.

It was quite obvious that the animal was playing a game.

No sooner did the groom reach his side and bend forward to take hold of the reins than he moved away, tantalizingly near, but just out of reach.

53

Calista gave another shrill whistle, a single note, and now without a moment's hesitation the animal came trotting up to her, the stirrup swinging as he moved.

She put out her hand, patted his neck and he nuzzled his nose against her cheek.

"Did you teach your horse these tricks?" the Earl asked.

"Of course," Calista answered. "He understands everything I say to him. That is why he is called 'Centaur'!"

"A creature half-horse, half-man!" the Earl smiled.

"I am glad to see you are more proficient in Greek than you are in good sense!" Calista remarked.

She looked beyond the Earl to where his stallion was trying to free himself from the bridle which held him to the post.

"What a magnificent horse!" she exclaimed in quite a different tone of voice.

"He is a new acquisition," the Earl said. "Had I realized the part I was expected to play this morning, I would have brought a quieter animal!"

He went towards the stallion as he spoke to untie him.

The horse reared up, his front hoofs

54

waving above the Earl's head.

He talked quietly to the animal and, after patting his neck, swung himself lithely into the saddle almost before the stallion realized what was happening.

He turned the horse round to find that Calista also had mounted.

"Thank you, Sir, for your kindness in assisting me," she said loudly and he realized she spoke for the groom's benefit.

"Bow to the gentleman, Centaur," she commanded.

To the Earl's surprise, her horse put out one front leg, bent the other and lowered his head.

Then without looking at the Earl again Calista rode away.

He watched her go, realizing that she had an excellent seat and rode superbly.

Then as he thought of what she had said to him, the strange way she had behaved, and the manner in which she had thrown herself from her horse at his feet, the Earl smiled.

"I must certainly discover what lies at the bottom of all this!" he told himself.

2

Lady Genevieve Rodney looked at the gown that was being held up for her by Madame Madeleine, the most expensive dressmaker in London, and could not repress a little cry of pleasure.

"It is ravishing!" she exclaimed.

"I was sure Your Ladyship would think so," Madame Madeleine replied. "It arrived only yesterday from Paris, and I knew as soon as I opened the box that it would suit Your Ladyship better than anyone else."

"I am sure it is very expensive," Lady Genevieve remarked a little doubtfully.

She knew that the lace which trimmed the off-the-shoulder *corsage à la grecque* and encircled in three deep flounces the full skirts and attached to the dress with knob roses, was the finest Venetian.

She was also well aware that the Earl had paid Madame Madeleine's outstanding and outrageous bill only the previous week.

Madame Madeleine astutely said nothing, but merely turned the gown round so that Lady Genevieve could see the soft satin ribbons of superlative quality which decorated the back.

Putting the gown down on the bed she produced another even more elaborate gown of *grôs de Chine* in a deep ruby red.

To offset the low cut bodice there were huge sleeves of silk and net while the tiny waist was encircled with velvet embroidered with diamanté. These also sparkled in the folds of the skirt and round the hem line.

"For very special occasions, Your Ladyship!" she said in an enticing tone, "perhaps for one of the three State Balls Her Majesty is giving to celebrate her Coronation?"

Lady Genevieve did not reply and after a moment Madame Madeleine went on:

"I hope I shall have the honour and privilege of making Your Ladyship's gown for the ceremony? Your Ladyship will undoubtedly stand out in the Abbey if I dress you in a gown that is sensational, especially as to colour."

There was a pause and then Lady Genevieve said:

"What colour would you think suitable?"

"The train-bearers, all unmarried young ladies," the dressmaker replied, "will wear white and silver dresses with silver wreaths trimmed with pink rosebuds in their hair. Very appropriate, I thought, when I learnt what had been chosen. But for you, My Lady. . ."

She paused and realizing that Lady Genevieve was listening attentively, went on:

"I thought a gown of gauze, peacock-blue, very low cut and moulded to Your Ladyship's beautiful bosom! An enormous skirt in green and blue shaded into each other and finished with a train edged with black ermine to match Your Ladyship's hair."

"It sounds intriguing," Lady Genevieve admitted.

"I had a little sketch drawn just to show Your Ladyship what I had in mind," Madame Madeleine said.

As she spoke she set down on the

dressing-table a sketch done by an artist who had skilfully portrayed Lady Genevieve's beautiful face and her lithe, slim body.

The sketch portrayed the sloping white shoulders which were the fashion and accentuated the caught-in waist, and the full skirts were framed by a train which Lady Genevieve was aware would be longer and more voluminous than those worn by any of the other Peeresses in the Abbey.

"It is very original!" she admitted, "and as you say, it would undoubtedly be sensational!"

"The green in the gown would go well with a tiara of emeralds and diamonds to match Your Ladyship's necklace," Madame Madeleine suggested. "Green makes Your Ladyship's eyes look mysterious and very provocative!"

Lady Genevieve laughed.

"Madame Madeleine, you are most persuasive, and indeed more encouraging than the Fortune-teller I visited in Maddock Street last week."

"I can tell your fortune, M'Lady, without looking at your palm," Madame Madeleine replied. "It is written in your face; for who else in the social world can hold a candle to you?"

lady Genevieve laughed again.

"Leave the sketch," she said, "the gown will doubtless be outrageously expensive, but if it makes the female guests in the Abbey grind their teeth and tear their hair with envy, it will be all due to you."

Madame Madeleine smiled.

"And the other gowns?" she asked softly.

"I will keep them both," Lady Genevieve replied, "but do not send in the bill for at least three weeks. You may have to wait longer."

"I am sure Your Ladyship does not have to trouble your head about money," Madame Madeleine said with an insinuation behind the words that was unmistakable.

She was well aware who paid the bills and she was too worldly-wise not to know that a lady had to wait for the right moment to ask for her bills to be met, especially when so much had been spent already.

"The gowns will fit Your Ladyship to

60

perfection," Madame Madelein continued. "The small alterations I thought necessary were attended to before I brought them here. If there is anything else that needs doing send me a message, M'Lady, and I will be with you as swiftly as my feet can carry me!"

"You are always very obliging, Madame Madeleine," Lady Genevieve said automatically.

Leaving the two gowns lying side by side on the satin cover of the bed Madame Madeleine bowed herself from the room and Lady Genevieve looked at herself in the mirror with a little smile of satisfaction.

She had been wondering what she should wear at the Coronation. She was determined that her presence would not go unnoticed.

People, she thought spitefully, were talking too much and over enthusing about that short, rather plain girl of nineteen who had just come to the throne.

There was of course no denying that the Queen enjoyed an unparalleled popularity among her Subjects and that her Ministers were determined to make the Coronation a day that the whole country would remember.

But it annoyed Lady Genevieve to know that while a mere £50,000 had been spent on the Coronation of the previous monarch, £200,000 had been voted by Parliament for the Coronation of Queen Victoria.

"What," she asked herself, "could I not do with a sum like that?"

Because Lady Genevieve liked always to hold the centre of the stage it irked her to hear people talk of little else except the ceremony which was to take place on the 28th June.

Westminster Abbey was to be magnificently decorated in crimson and gold. A two-day Fair on a huge scale with balloon ascents was to be arranged in Hyde Park, and there were also to be illuminations and firework displays.

"If you ask me, it is a ridiculous waste of money!" Lady Genevieve had said on several occasions, only to find that no-one was prepared to agree with her.

Her friends were concerned with nothing but their own appearance and dressmakers had been besieged by clients eager for new ideas, new materials, regardless of cost.

Lady Genevieve had deliberately delayed ordering her own gown until she had some idea of what her rivals would be wearing.

She wanted to outshine them all and she knew that her small waist, her ivory-white shoulders and flawless skin must be displayed at their best; for although her jewels were very fine they could easily be overshadowed by those worn by the Duchesses and Marchionesses who owned family jewels that had been accumulated for generations.

Lady Genevieve knew she must plan both her appearance and her entrance, and it was not only the vast crowd of socialites that she wished to impress, but also one Peer in particular — the Earl of Helstone.

At the thought of him there was a slight frown between her large dark eyes and her red mouth pouted a little.

He was not an easy man to handle, in fact by far the most difficult she had ever known; but she had made up her mind to marry him and she was determined to get her own way.

'If our engagement were to be announced before the Coronation,' she thought, 'it would be an added feather in my cap if he escorted me up the aisle to my seat.'

She was well aware that the 'Elusive Earl' was proving more than usually elusive, but she was supremely confident that he would not escape her and she had in fact played her trump-card when he had been with her the night before he left for the Newmarket races.

She thought of his great possessions, of his house in Piccadilly where she would entertain the *Beau Monde*. When they stood together at the top of the double staircase it would be indisputable that no host could look more handsome and no hostess more beautiful.

Then there was his Mansion in Surrey. Even to think of it made Lady Genevieve draw in her breath appreciatively.

What parties she would give there! There would be Balls in the summer with the long windows of the Salons opening out onto rose-gardens which scented the air.

She could see herself moving through

the magnificent apartments with their painted ceilings and huge crystal chandeliers, descending the carved stairway with its heraldic newels, or wandering down the long Picture Gallery where her portrait would join those of the other Countesses of Helstone.

"That is what I want; that would be the perfect setting for me," she told herself and smiled at her own reflection in the mirror.

There was a knock on the door and one of her maids entered.

The girl curtsied a little nervously to the back of her mistress's head and wondered what sort of temper she was in.

Lady Genevieve was unpredictable and her maids were well aware that a well-aimed hairbrush could be very painful.

"What is it?" Lady Genevieve asked sharply after nearly a minute had passed.

"The Prime Minister has called, M'Lady."

Lady Genevieve started to her feet.

"The Prime Minister? Why did you not say so at once, you nit-wit?"

She turned to have a quick glance at herself in the mirror and was well satisfied with what she saw, realizing that the négligée she wore, although it was late in the morning, did little to conceal the curves of her almost perfect figure.

The maid held open the door and she passed through it and went slowly down the narrow staircase to the Drawing-Room on the first floor where Viscount Melbourne was waiting.

He was a distant cousin and had been a close friend of Lady Genevieve's father, the Duke of Harrogate. Lady Genevieve had known him and loved him since she was a child.

When she entered the Drawing-Room and saw Lord Melbourne waiting for her, she ran towards him with a little cry of delight.

At fifty-nine, the Prime Minister was still a remarkably handsome man.

He had in his youth possessed dazzling good looks, his eyes and the set of his head being particularly admired.

He liked the society of women and was extremely attracted to them.

His social talents were exceptional and his wit was invariably unique and entertaining.

He was extremely sophisticated and experienced, and there was a glint of admiration and amusement in his eyes when he saw how Lady Genevieve was dressed.

She reached his side, put her arms round his neck and kissed his cheek.

"Cousin William, how sweet of you to come!" she said. "I knew you would answer my note, but I did not expect to see you so quickly!"

"You know if you need help," Lord Melbourne replied, "I am always there to give it to you."

"Thank you!" Lady Genevieve said, and taking her arms from around his neck she put her hand in his and drew him down beside her on the sofa.

"Will you have some refreshment?" she asked. "A glass of Madeira, or champagne, if you would prefer it?"

"I want nothing," Lord Melbourne answered, "except to look at you!"

His smile was irresistible as he continued:

"You are in great good looks, my dear. I know of no-one else who could be so outstandingly beautiful at this hour of the morning."

"Thank you, Cousin William!" Lady Genevieve said. "And now, kindest of all men, I need your help."

Lord Melbourne raised his eyebrows and waited.

"It is of course an oversight — I am aware of that," Lady Genevieve said, "but I have not received my invitation to the Coronation."

Almost as if he was unconscious of doing so, Lord Melbourne released his hand and raised it reflectively to his chin.

He did not look at Lady Genevieve as he said quietly:

"It is not an oversight!"

There was a moment's silence, before she said in an incredulous tone:

"You mean I am not to be invited?"

"The Queen has crossed out your name on the list that was presented to her."

"I cannot believe it!" Lady Genevieve said in a stifled tone. "How can she dare . . . how can she presume. . .?"

Her voice faded away and Lord Melbourne gave a little sigh.

"You have, my dear, been somewhat indiscreet."

"You mean . . . with Osric Helstone?"

"He is one of many, but perhaps your association with him and the way it has been talked about has brought things to a head."

"You mean it has annoyed those catty old women, those frowsty old Dowagers, who had been angling over him for their pi-faced daughters for years, determined that if they cannot get hold of him, no-one else shall?" Lady Genevieve stormed and her eyes were flashing.

"You may have a point there," Lord Melbourne agreed. "At the same time, my dear, as I warned you only a little while ago, times have changed. What was permitted in the gay Regency days and enjoyed by George IV when he was on the throne, is now frowned upon most severely!"

There was a faint smile on his lips, as if he were recalling how he himself had enjoyed the loose, raffish society of those days, when the ladies were nearly as free in their behaviour as the gentlemen.

"King William and Queen Adelaide, as you know," he went on, "did their best to improve both manners and morals."

Lady Genevieve laughed scornfully.

"The King was hardly the right person to do that," she said, "considering he had ten bastards by Mrs. Jordan!"

"Nevertheless," Lord Melbourne replied, "he set new standards of behaviour and most people conformed."

He looked at Lady Genevieve in a meaning way as he spoke and she smiled at him.

"I never was a conformer!"

"I know that," he answered, "but you must understand that the Queen is very young, very innocent, and very good!"

Lady Genevieve was just about to say something scathing when she remembered that the whole world believed that Lord Melbourne was in love with the Queen.

She certainly adored him, and the man who had been a sophisticated wit and cited as co-respondent in two divorce cases, had nevertheless emerged miraculously unscathed and was now prepared to trim his brilliance, his scepticism and cynicism to suit her innocent ears.

To his friends it seemed incredible that he could bring himself to endure the long evenings with the young Queen, playing

70

School-room games, like draughts, and putting together dissected pictures.

Lady Genevieve had even heard that when he talked about Queen Victoria the Prime Minister's eyes filled with tears.

She had not believed it, but now instead of the attack she had intended to make on the young Queen she said:

"Surely you can persuade Her Majesty, Cousin William, that it would be an overwhelming insult, resented by every member of my family, if I were to be excluded from the Coronation?"

She knew even as she spoke that it was not a very convincing argument.

Her father was dead, her mother lived in the depths of Dorset and never came to Court. Her other relatives, and there were quite a number of them, disapproved of her and far from being affronted would undoubtedly be delighted if she was given a social 'set-down'.

Quickly, because she knew that Lord Melbourne was not impressed, Lady Genevieve said:

"I have a better case than that! I am to marry Osric Helstone!"

Lord Melbourne looked at her searchingly.

"The 'Elusive Earl'?" he queried. "Are you sure?"

"Quite sure!"

"That of course would alter everything," he said. "At the same time, has Helstone actually asked you to be his wife?"

Lady Genevieve's eyes were unable to meet his.

"Not in so many words," she admitted, "but he will."

"I wish for your sake I could be sure of that," Lord Melbourne said quietly.

He rose from the sofa as he spoke and walked to the mantelshelf to lean against it with an elegance that was peculiarly his own.

After a moment he said:

"I have known you, Genevieve, since you were in your cradle. Your father was one of my dearest friends, and your mother was very kind to me at a time in my life when I was exceedingly unhappy."

Lady Genevieve knew he was referring to the time when he had married against the wishes of his family, the lovely, eccentric and wilful Lady Caroline Ponsonby, only daughter of the Earl of Bessborough, and she had created a public scandal by her passion for Lord Byron.

She had died ten years ago in 1828, and Lady Genevieve's mother had often spoken of the years of patience, forbearance and forgiveness that Lord Melbourne had shown his wife before she became uncontrollably excitable and finally insane.

He had not only suffered that unhappiness, but their only child, a son named Augustus, proved to be feeble-minded and died a year after his mother.

"Papa and Mama always loved you," Lady Genevieve said now, "as I have."

"Then I wish you would sometimes listen to the warnings I have given you," Lord Melbourne said.

Lady Genevieve shrugged her shoulders.

"Life is short and I wish to enjoy myself."

"Women can be very cruel to a woman who is more beautiful than they are, and who offends the social rules."

"We were talking about Osric," Lady Genevieve said quickly.

"I know," Lord Melbourne answered,

"and I hope for your sake that you are able to bring him up to scratch where a large number of lovely women have failed to do so. But I think, Genevieve, you forget one thing."

"What is that?" Lady Genevieve asked almost in a hostile tone.

"A man will amuse himself — and who will blame him — when women are attracted to him and he is attracted by them. But from his wife he expects something more than the satisfaction of desire."

"What do you mean by that?"

"I mean," Lord Melbourne continued as if he were feeling for words, "that a man wants his wife to be pure and untouched. I think every man has an ideal within his heart of what he requires from the woman who will bear his name."

"Pure and untouched?" Lady Genevieve repeated incredulously.

She was just about to laugh jeeringly when she realized that in fact that was what Lord Melbourne had sought in Caroline Ponsonby and what he loved in the Queen.

There had, she knew, been many women

in his life, but she realized now that he was an idealist who found something spiritual in an immature woman, young, unsophisticated and child-like.

Fighting back the words she would have said, Lady Genevieve remarked:

"It is a little late in the day for you to expect me to be as I was when I came out at seventeen."

"That is true," Lord Melbourne agreed, "and Helstone may find your recklessness, your flaunting of the conventions, the devilment which lurks in your eyes very attractive. But are you quite certain that he wants those things in his wife?"

"He will marry me," Lady Genevieve said obstinately.

Lord Melbourne gave a little sigh.

"In which case there is nothing more for me to say. My lecture is at an end, my dear."

He spoke beguilingly and Lady Genevieve rose to her feet to move towards him and lay her hands on his shoulders.

"If Osric marries me, Cousin William, I will do my best to settle down and behave more circumspectly. As his wife, I certainly could not be excluded from

Court."

"Not if you behave yourself," Lord Melbourne agreed.

"I shall do that," Lady Genevieve promised. "And now will you get me invited to the Coronation?"

"That is impossible," Lord Melbourne replied, "unless of course your engagement to the Earl is announced before June 28th."

Lady Genevieve's lips tightened.

"That gives me a deadline, does it not? Well, I shall do my damnedest, you can be sure of that!"

"And try not to swear," Lord Melbourne begged. "The Queen, like most young girls, is extremely shocked if anyone uses a swear-word in her presence."

"How can you bear it, Cousin William?" Lady Genevieve asked. "You, of all people!"

Lord Melbourne paused before he replied:

"I think now that all I have learnt in my life, all the knowledge I have accumulated and all I have suffered, was meant to be utilized in training a young woman, who I am convinced, will be a great

Queen."

"Do you really believe that?"

"I believe it!" he said simply. "And what is more, she believes in me!"

Lady Genevieve was silent.

She remembered that someone had told her that the Queen had described Lord Melbourne as the 'best hearted, the kindest and the most feeling man in the world'!

Lady Genevieve, when he left, having kissed her tenderly good-bye, picked up an ornament which stood on a table in the Hall and smashed it to pieces on the ground.

She then cursed, loudly and violently, the social world, the prying slanderous old women who were part of it, and those who had carried tales of her indiscretions to the Queen.

The footmen heard her with pale faces and frightened eyes, while the maid-servants who were peeping round the bedroom door at the top of the staircase giggled amongst themselves.

Still swearing, Lady Genevieve walked upstairs and back to her bedroom, where she vented her anger still further by slapping the face of her younger maid and by hitting the older one with a hairbrush until she burst into tears.

She was, however, smiling and looking extremely and beguilingly beautiful when half an hour later she was informed that the Earl of Helstone had called to see her.

She walked into the Drawing-Room wearing a new gown of embroidered muslin trimmed with bows of velvet and carrying on her arm a shawl of *grôs de Naples* garnished with lace. In her hand she held a high poke bonnet trimmed with cock feathers, with a lace inset which would encircle her whole face and fall in frills beneath her small chin.

Lord Helstone looking extremely elegant in a cut-away coat with wide revers, his high collar very white against his square chin, was standing where Lord Melbourne had stood, in front of the fireplace.

Looking at him Lady Genevieve thought for the first time that the two men had something in common.

They both had an air of ease and confidence.

Lady Genevieve had heard it called

'insouciance' but she thought it was the manner in which they faced life with the air of one who is always in command of a situation, never nonplussed by anything that might occur, however dramatic.

Lady Genevieve closed the door behind her and stood still to look at Lord Helstone on the other side of the room.

She knew he would take in the elegance of her gown, the Grecian angle at which she carried her head, and the fact that the sunlight revealed the deep blue and dark purple lights in the beauty of her hair.

"I have been longing to see you, Osric!" she said at length in her most beguiling tone.

"I want to talk to you, Genevieve."

Lady Genevieve moved towards the Earl.

"Are words so important?" she asked as she reached his side, lifting her face to his.

He looked down at her and his eyes were hard.

"Sit down, Genevieve. There are certain things we must discuss."

He thought there was a flicker of uncertainty in her eyes. But she gave a little shrug of her shoulders, pouted her lips and seated herself gracefully on the sofa.

"I am waiting," she said after a moment, and there was a defiant note in her voice.

"The last time I saw you," the Earl said, "you told me you were carrying my child."

Lady Genevieve smiled. "That is true," she said. "I thought it would please you — an heir to carry on the family name. Is not that what every man requires?"

"In certain circumstances — yes," the Earl agreed. "But I wish of course to be sure the child is mine."

Lady Genevieve opened her eyes very wide.

"Osric, how can you doubt such a thing? You must know there has been no-one else in my life since we loved each other. You are everything to me, everything! How could you imagine that I would even look at another man?"

"There is also something else of great importance."

"What is that?"

"I would like to be absolutely sure that you are in fact *enceinte*."

"How can you question it? Of course it is early days, but a woman always knows these things, and I am certain, quite certain, that I shall give you a son."

Her voice was very soft and sweet as she asked:

"How soon can we be married? I would not wish to leave it too long."

"No, I agree with you, that is very important," the Earl replied. "That is why, if you will put on your bonnet, I suggest we call immediately on Sir James Clark."

"Sir James Clark?" Lady Genevieve enquired. "Who is he?"

"He is physician to the Queen and a gynaecologist of great repute."

There was a moment's silence. Then Lady Genevieve said:

"It is too early to be making arrangements of that sort. I see no point in troubling the Doctor at this moment. I feel well—in fact I have never felt better!"

"What I require Sir James Clark to tell me," the Earl explained, "is whether in fact you are with child. If you are, I will consider marrying you."

Lady Genevieve's eyes met his.

"I see no reason why I should submit myself to such an indignity," she said defiantly.

"Why not tell the truth?" the Earl asked. "You well know there is no child, nor is there ever likely to be."

She did not answer, but he was aware of the questions running through her mind: should she lie to him, storm at him, or even agree to his assertion?

"I happen to know," he said before she could speak, "that it is impossible for you to have a baby. You tried to give Rodney an heir and failed!"

"Who has told you this?" Lady Genevieve began angrily, then gave a little exclamation. "Of course I know who has been saying such things — Willoughby Yaxley! He must have listened to that sneaking, spiteful sister of his. I always did loathe Louise!"

"Nevertheless she was speaking the truth!"

"Very well then—I am not having a baby at the moment!" Lady Genevieve said angrily. "But that is no reason to be certain that I shall never have one!"

The Earl drew an envelope from the

inside pocket of his coat and laid it on the mantelpiece.

"What is that?" she asked somewhat apprehensively.

"It is a cheque," he replied, "for a sum of money which will certainly cover your expenses up to today. Good-bye, Genevieve!"

"Good-bye?" she echoed, her voice rising. "Are you leaving me? You cannot mean to do such a thing!"

"If there is one thing I dislike it is being lied to and tricked," the Earl said coldly. "I am only sorry that our acquaintance should end on such an unpleasant note. It was not of my seeking."

"You cannot mean it!" Lady Genevieve cried.

She rose from the sofa and went towards the Earl.

"I love you, Osric, you know that! If I have lied, if I have tried to inveigle you into marriage, it is only because I love you."

"And you really think such a lie would be a good foundation on which to build our married life?" the Earl enquired.

He laughed, but there was no humour

in it.

"You have only confirmed my determination to stay single and that so-called 'marriage bliss' is not for me!"

Lady Genevieve tried to put her arms round his neck, but he took her by both wrists and released himself.

"There is nothing more to be said!" he remarked and walked towards the door.

She ran after him frantically.

"Please, Osric, listen to me! I will explain! I will tell you why I said such a thing. You must try to understand. . ."

"I understand perfectly!" the Earl said and his voice was hard. He opened the door, let himself out and walked down the stairs.

"Osric, stay with me! Let us talk about it . . . please. . ."

Lady Genevieve was leaning over the banisters and the last word was a shrill scream as the footman handed the Earl his hat and cane and opened the door for him.

He did not look back, he only set his tall hat on his head and walked out into the street.

Lady Genevieve stared at the closed

door.

For once she was past swearing; past uttering any expression of her feelings.

.   .   .

Back in his own house the Earl was conscious of feeling free and unencumbered in a manner which gave him more relief than he had ever experienced before when an *affaire-de-cœur* was over.

It was always difficult to say good-bye, to finish what had been a close intimacy with a sharp blow, rather than let it peter out when neither partner was any longer infatuated with the other.

The Earl could be very ruthless when it suited him, and he was never sentimental about his relationships. But he disliked more than anything else the female recriminations which so often accompanied the parting of the ways.

He thought now that he had in fact begun to grow tired of Lady Genevieve, even before he was infuriated and disgusted by her attempt to trick him into marriage.

She could, it was true, excite his desires;

but he found once the fire had burnt itself out that she left him with a sense of disillusionment and dissatisfaction.

Once again he told himself that beauty was not enough.

It would be difficult to imagine anyone could be more beautiful than Lady Genevieve, but he had sensed that her character was an unpleasant one, and it had certainly been far more expensive to satisfy her greed than that of any other woman with whom he had associated before.

He felt now he had more than paid his way and that the very generous cheque he had left on her mantelpiece would keep her in ample comfort until she found another protector to meet her bills.

He told himself with some surprise that he felt no guilt of any sort where Lady Genevieve was concerned.

Sometimes when he left a woman weeping he had felt sorry to have captured her heart to such a point that it must ache for a long time after he had gone.

But he was quite certain that if Genevieve had a heart it was not involved to any great extent where he was concerned.

He had always known that it was

impossible to consider a man in isolation from the position he occupied or the possessions he owned.

When he was very young he had thought that one day he would find a woman who would love him for himself alone, who would not care whether he was heir to an Earldom and a vast fortune, or dependent entirely on his own wits.

But soon he knew that such a female phenomenon did not exist.

Once or twice he had believed that it was in fact just for himself that two beautiful eyes looked soft and emotional and two red lips sought his.

But while there was no doubt that women fell in love with him and loved him wholeheartedly, he could never be sure, handsome and attractive though he might be, that it was for himself alone.

"Oh, Osric, I love you!"

"I love you, I love you!"

How often had he heard those words whispered in the darkness when a woman lay in his arms, and he had wanted to believe that they were spoken for him because he was the lover of their dreams.

And yet always, when daylight came,

there had been that faint suggestion, usually very tactfully put, of the gems that were most becoming or the bill that remained unpaid for the delectable gown which he had admired.

"Perhaps I have been unfortunate," the Earl told himself sometimes, "or else I have moved in the wrong type of society."

Then he laughed at himself and thought that perhaps his mother had told him too many fairy-tales when he was a child, and that deep down in his mind there was the story of the goose-girl who had married the Prince, or the ragged maiden who fell in love with the valet, having no idea that he was in fact a Prince in disguise.

"I am what I am!" he told himself firmly, "and because of it I must expect women to take me at my face value!"

And yet in Helstone House, surrounded by his possessions, he had the depressing feeling that all women were very much like Genevieve.

"Liars and cheats!" he said aloud and found Mr. Grotham at his elbow.

"You spoke, My Lord?"

"To myself," the Earl replied.

Mr. Grotham handed him a list of his

engagements for the next two days.

The Earl glanced at them, then said sharply:

"Cancel them all — I intend to go to the country!"

"To the country, My Lord?"

"Yes. There are things to be attended to, and for the moment I am bored with London!"

"Very good, My Lord. Will you require your Phaeton in which to travel? And I will send a groom ahead of you immediately so that everything is in readiness for your arrival."

"I will leave in half an hour," the Earl said.

Mr. Grotham hurried from the room.

However, the Earl found his ancestral country home, which was redolent with his ancestors, seemed empty and unnaturally quiet.

He could not help feeling that it was a house that should be filled with a large family, and not only children but those who attended them; Nurses, Governesses, Tutors and Teachers of every sort, and he thought too it was time he entertained the County and took upon himself the many commitments which had occupied his father's time.

That evening after dinner he walked onto the terrace. It was a warm night and the last dying light of the sun was a crimson glory behind the ancient oak trees.

It was so beautiful that the Earl suddenly longed for someone with whom to share it. He thought of Genevieve but knew he would never have lived with her fiery and insatiable passion in the house where his mother had reigned so severely.

In complete contrast there could be someone young and innocent like the Queen.

Then the Earl remembered that Charles Greville, Clerk to the Privy Council and celebrated diarist had shown him what he had recorded with 'accurate fidelity' as an example of conversation at Court.

The Queen: "Have you been riding to-
    day, Mr. Greville?"
Charles Greville: "No, Madam, I have
    not."
The Queen: "It is a fine day."
Charles Greville: "Yes, Ma'am, a very

fine day."

The Queen: "It is rather cold, though."

Charles Greville: (like Polonius) "It *was* rather cold, Madame."

The Queen: "Your sister, Lady Francis Egerton, rides I think, does she not?"

Charles Greville: "She does ride sometimes, Madam."

The Earl read it and laughed, but now he said to himself:

"It would be intolerable! I could not endure such insipid banality."

After two or three days of riding around the farms, visiting his tenants, discussing improvements with his Agent and exercising his horses, the Earl returned to London.

"Where on earth have you been Osric?" Lord Yaxley asked when he called at Helstone House to find the owner had returned.

"I was required in the country," the Earl replied.

"Good God, at this time of the year? You missed the Richmond's Ball which was attended by the Queen and there have been some amusing dinner-parties

91

from which you were notably absent!"

"I am glad people were aware that I was not present," the Earl said.

"Of course, when the news appeared today, everybody thought you were suffering from an aching heart," Lord Yaxley remarked.

"What news?" the Earl enquired.

"You do not know?"

"What should I know?"

"That Genevieve has announced her engagement to Lord Bowden."

As he spoke Lord Yaxley was watching the Earl's face, but it was expressionless.

"You are surprised?" he asked after a moment.

"No!" the Earl answered. "I knew that Bowden has been pursuing her for a year."

"He is over sixty!" Lord Yaxley said. "And one of the biggest bores it has ever been my misfortune to meet!"

The Earl thought the same but he did not say so.

He surmised various explanations but he did not know that the real reason lay in the fact that Lady Genevieve was determined to attend the Coronation.

It was three days later that Lord Yaxley found himself being driven with the Earl's outstanding expertise towards Epsom.

When they were out of the traffic, the Earl said:

"Tell me about our hostess, Lady Chevington. I really know very little about her although if you remember, we stayed for two nights at Chevington Court last year."

"I remember it well," Lord Yaxley said. "It was the worst Derby I have ever experienced—financially, I mean."

"I made money," the Earl replied. "If you would only follow my advice, Willoughby, you would fare better on the racecourse."

"I know that!" Lord Yaxley snapped, "but the truth is, Osric, I get carried away by the enthusiasm of my other friends who are always so completely sure their horses will come romping home to beat yours, and as the odds are invariably much better, I am tempted!"

"Then at this meeting, listen to me!" the Earl said with a smile.

"I will," Lord Yaxley promised. "What was it you wanted to know about Lady

Chevington?"

"Tell me about her."

"Well, you probably know that her husband, Sir Hugo, who died some years ago, was without exception the most charming and popular man who ever crossed the threshold of White's. My father used to say that, if he had to pick out the nicest, kindest and most delightful person he had ever met, he would unhesitatingly point to Hugo Chevington."

"I remember him," Lord Helstone said, "although he was of course much older than I."

"He was quite old when he married for the first time," Lord Yaxley said. "He fell in love with the wife of Sir Joseph Harkney, an enormously rich businessman and never looked at anyone else."

"Businessman?" the Earl queried sharply.

"Harkney was in shipping, I believe, which is more respectable and certainly more acceptable than the City, but he was definitely not the *crème de la crème*, if you know what I mean."

"I know exactly!" the Earl agreed.

"Well, apparently Eleanor Harkney

was the most beautiful creature that anyone had ever seen. She is still very good
looking."

"Yes, I suppose she is," the Earl
remarked.

"She is also extremely intelligent and
very ambitious."

The Earl waited and Lord Yaxley went
on:

"She certainly expended her money
very skilfully once Harkney died and Sir
Hugo married her. She set out to make
the world forget who she had been and
where she came from. At least, that is
what my father always said."

"And has obviously been very successful!" the Earl remarked, remembering
the notables he had met the last time he
had stayed at Chevington Court.

"Poor old Sir Hugo never had much
money," Lord Yaxley went on, "but he
loved racing and Lady Chevington bought
that enormous mansion at Epsom from
an impoverished nobleman who could not
afford its upkeep.

"With Sir Hugo as host, there was no-
one from the Royal family downwards
who would refuse to be entertained with

every luxurious comfort."

Lord Yaxley paused.

"Go on!" the Earl prompted. "You tell a story well, Willoughby, I can see exactly what happened."

"A large house in London and a Castle in Scotland with a really good grouse-moor completed the parcel," Lord Yaxley said. "When Sir Hugo died, Lady Chevington made quite sure she was still *persona grata* in society by having first a Duke and then a Marquis as sons-in-law."

"Are the Chevington girls pretty?" the Earl enquired.

"Pretty and rich!"

"So there was no question of Frampton and Northaw being pressured into marriage?"

Lord Yaxley considered the question.

"I should not think so," he answered. "Personally I would not want to marry Frampton if I were a girl and I always think Northaw is to let in the attics. But one never knows where a woman's fancy lies."

"That is true!" the Earl agreed.

"I wonder who will be in the house-party?" Lord Yaxley went on. "It is sure to be entertaining. Lady Chevington has the wisdom to mix her guests intelligently. If you invite nothing but Politicians, or nothing but gamblers, or nothing but society idiots, they soon become bored with each other and themselves! It is variety which makes a good party—I am sure of it."

"And into which category do you think we fall?" the Earl enquired.

Lord Yaxley laughed.

"I am undoubtedly a 'social idiot', but you Osric, are in a class of your own, rather like your horses! Is Delos going to win the Derby?"

"If I were you I should certainly put a little money on him," the Earl said.

"That means he is!" Lord Yaxley said.

"We will go and look at him early tomorrow morning."

"I am told that Arkrie fancies his animal's chances. If you pip him at the post once again, he will have a stroke!"

"That would undoubtedly be a most regrettable occurrence!" the Earl said sarcastically.

But he was smiling as he drove on.

3

There was certainly every evidence of an abundance of money, the Earl thought, at Chevington Court.

The house itself was enormous but not particularly attractive. It had been added to at various times in its history, yet unlike many other old houses it had acquired a 'patched' appearance instead of a harmonious whole.

The main structure was however only a hundred years old with huge rooms, lofty ceilings and magnificent mantelshelves.

The Earl thought when they entered the oval Hall that he had never seen such an army of servants, all somewhat spectacularly dressed in a claret-coloured livery with a large amount of gold braid.

He realized he was being more observant and perhaps more critical than he had been on his previous visit simply because of Calista's extraordinary warning to him.

As Lady Chevington glided across the Salon to greet him, he recalled all that Lord Yaxley had told him about her.

It was obvious she must have been very beautiful and she still was an amazingly good-looking woman.

She had an art of making every man she talked to feel he was the one person with whom she wished to have a conversation. And there was no doubt that she intended to make her guests comfortable.

There was nothing, the Earl thought later that evening, that had been forgotten or overlooked which could make a visitor feel he was a pampered and valued person.

Every published newspaper was brought to every male guest's bedroom when he was called in the morning. They had been brought from London by a relay of fast horses, the first of which left at dawn.

There was a selection of three button-holes on every man's dressing-table to choose from before he went down to dinner.

And for the ladies there were elaborate and very beautiful corsages which they could either pin in the front of their low cut gowns or carry in their hands.

Although the Earl had brought his own personal valet with him, there was another valet in attendance on him alone, and he knew that in no other establishment would his horses or grooms be so well looked after.

It was interesting to find that the house-party was extremely distinguished.

The first person he saw was the Dictator of the Turf, Lord George Cavendish Bentinck. The Dictators had a most important part to play in giving an undisputed ruling over any controversy and seeing that the rules of the Jockey Club were followed down to the most minute detail.

Lord George Bentinck who had been an Etonian and a Life Guard, was a handsome man with whom the Earl had many interests in common.

He was sensitive and haughty, agreeable yet domineering, able and untiring, a loyal friend but an extremely vindictive enemy.

Unlike the Earl he was however a heavy gambler and had lost £27,000 when Lord Scarborough's Tarrare won the St. Leger in 1826.

Nevertheless he proved himself so knowledgeable about horses that a year later his brother guaranteed him £300,000 with which to start a stable.

The Earl was also delighted to find that the Foreign Secretary, Lord Palmerston, was one of the guests.

Lord Palmerston was in fact very much older than the Earl, but he had a youthfulness about him which made him friends with people of different ages and varying types.

He had the loud, yattering laugh of a self-confident Whig, a robust temper and a gay taste in waistcoats and women!

With women he was always enterprising and audacious and everyone was well aware that the Queen, fortunately, knew nothing of her Foreign Secretary's nocturnal wanderings at Windsor Castle.

There were several important members of Parliament besides, as might be expected, a number of the most prominent noblemen in the racing world.

After a quick scrutiny of the guests the Earl was quite certain that he was going to enjoy himself, and he was further assured of this when he saw in the party many beautiful and charming married women, some of whom had already been his flirts in the past.

There were very few young people with the exception of Lady Chevington's two daughters, the Duchess of Frampton and the Marchioness of Northaw, with their husbands, and of course Calista.

She was not to be seen when the Earl and Lord Yaxley arrived, but she was in the Salon when the Earl came down for dinner.

He was looking extremely dashing in his exquisitely cut evening-dress which set off his athletic figure and practically every woman in the room looked at him with an appreciative eye as he moved to his hostess's side.

She introduced him to several people he had not already met and then said, with what he fancied was a special note in her voice:

"I do not think you have met my daughter, Calista?"

Calista curtsied and the Earl bowed.

He had not been mistaken, he realized, in thinking when he had first seen Calista, that she was very lovely.

She was wearing an elegant gown of white and silver, just demure enough for a débutante but having that extra chic which only money could buy.

Her hair, arranged in long ringlets on either side of her small pointed face, glinted with fiery tints of red in the light from the chandeliers, but the Earl saw that her grey-green eyes had a scornful expression in them when she looked at him.

She turned away before they exchanged a single word, but the Earl confidently expected he would be seated next to her.

To his surprise Calista was the other side of the table and he found himself being amusingly and wittily entertained by the wife of an elderly Peer who had engaged his attention for a brief and fiery interlude two years earlier.

The food, as he might have expected, was superlative. There was a footman behind every chair and an epicure would have found it difficult to fault the wine.

When dinner was over the gentlemen lingered for a long time in the Dining-Room over their port, and when finally they joined the ladies in the Salon the Earl noticed that Calista was not present.

"The whole story of her mother's intention is just a figment of adolescent imagination," he told himself as he sat down at the card-table and dismissed her from his mind.

As there was to be a long day's racing the following day, the ladies retired early to bed; but the Earl sat discussing horses and probable winners until after midnight.

Finally, almost reluctantly, because the conversation had been so interesting, the Earl went to his bedroom and after having a few words with Lord Yaxley shut the door.

The Earl was peculiar in that he disliked having a valet waiting up for him. It was usual for any nobleman in his position to have one, if not two servants to help him out of his evening-clothes; to assist him into his nightshirt; and finally to extinguish the lights once he was in bed.

The Earl found such attention irritating.

"I always waited up for your father, M'Lord," his senior valet had protested.

"My father was an old man when he died and doubtless he needed your assistance, Travers," the Earl said. "I find it disturbing to remember when I am very late that you have to be later still."

"It's part of my duty, M'Lord."

"That is for me to decide," the Earl replied. "When I want you to wait up for me I will say so—or I will ring the bell. Otherwise you will leave everything ready and I will attend to myself."

He knew that his valets were scandalized by his independence, feeling they had lost face amongst the other staff. While they stayed away from him they feared they might be accused of not looking after their master properly.

But the Earl was adamant.

Sometimes when he reached his bedroom he would sit reading before he undressed, and he knew that to have a valet hovering in the background would be an unnecessary irritation.

Now as he walked across his bedroom he thought how attractive it was.

He had not been put in the new more impressive part of Chevington Court but in what was known as the 'Elizabethan

Wing', which had a charm all its own.

It had in fact been the main part of the original house. Outside the walls were weathered red brick with gabled windows.

Inside the ceilings were low, the four-posters were of oak, and many of the walls were panelled with wood which had mellowed over the years to a beautiful ash-brown.

The room seemed hot and the Earl walked to the bow-window to pull back the closed curtain preparatory to opening a diamond-paned casement.

As he did so he heard a low whistle.

It was the same sound he had heard Calista utter when she gave her orders to Centaur, and the Earl leaned out of the window to look into the garden.

It was a clear night, the stars were brilliant in the velvet darkness of the sky, and the half-moon high overhead cast its silver light over the lake below the house and gave the gardens an ethereal beauty which the Earl had not noticed about them in the day-time.

He could see the lawn beneath his window quite clearly and there was no-one on it.

The whistle sounded again and now he realized it came from a huge magnolia tree whose white, wax-like flowers were close against his window.

He looked and saw that in the centre of the branches, perched so high in the tree that she was almost level with him, was Calista!

"I want to talk to you!"

He could hardly hear the words, they were spoken in so low a voice. But he leant out of the window to ask:

"What about?"

"About yourself. I told you not to come here."

"It is rather difficult to have a conversation in such circumstances," the Earl said. "Perhaps I had better join you."

"You would never manage it!" she said scathingly. "It is easier to climb from this tree into the house than vice versa."

The Earl looked at magnolia tree appraisingly. It was very old but its branches looked strong and he knew they would hold his weight.

His bedroom was on the first floor and it was not a very great distance to the ground.

He climbed up onto the window only to hear Calista say quickly:

"You had much better not attempt this. I would not wish you to fall and hurt yourself and for me to be responsible for it."

"I am not entirely decrepit," the Earl replied sharply.

It somehow annoyed him that this young girl should think him incapable of climbing down a tree.

It was in fact quite difficult to move round the open casement to the branch nearest to him, but the Earl was far more agile than the majority of his friends.

Fencing, boxing, and riding kept him in the peak of condition, and once he had reached the main trunk of the magnolia tree he found it easy to climb to the ground.

It certainly did not improve the appearance of his evening-breeches, but otherwise he reached it without mishap, Calista having descended ahead of him.

He stood for a moment wiping his hands before she said:

"As you are here we had best get out of sight of the windows, although Mama sleeps the other side of the house."

She moved quickly as she spoke into some thick rhododendron bushes which bordered the lawn. In the centre of them the Earl found a twisting, narrow path.

Following her he realized almost with a feeling of shock that she was wearing a pair of the tight, knitted pantaloons that had been so popular with the arbiters of fashion in the reign of George IV.

Above them she had on what the Earl guessed was a jockey's coat. It was the blue of the servants' livery, but was completed with primrose-yellow collar and cuffs.

The Earl remembered it was in fact the Chevington racing colours.

They moved on without speaking until suddenly the rhododendrons came to an end and they had reached the edge of the lake.

There was a seat almost hidden by a great arch of honeysuckle. The Earl knew as Calista sat down that it would be quite impossible for them to be seen by anyone who was not directly in front of them.

The lake was an enchantment of silver and on the other side stretched the parkland with stags clustered at the foot of the trees.

In the moonlight it was easy to see Calista's face and the Earl with a faint smile on his lips, said as he looked at her:

"Is not the fact that we are alone here together already somewhat compromising? Could it not play directly into your mother's hands?"

"Mama has taken her usual drops of laudanum," Calista answered, "and will be quite oblivious to anything we are doing at this particular moment."

"What did you want to say to me?"

"I want to tell you to be very careful. You have ignored my warning about coming to stay, so for goodness sake be on your guard."

"I have come to the conclusion that you are imagining the whole situation," the Earl replied. "I am not denying that your mother might be ready to welcome me as a son-in-law, but I cannot believe that she would do anything out of the ordinary to bring it about."

Calista gave a little laugh.

"How do you think Ambrosine got such a distinguished husband?"

There was a sarcastic note in her voice and the Earl, remembering that the Duke had imbibed so freely at dinner that he had had to be helped from the Dining-Room, was silent.

"I will tell you," Calista went on as he did not answer. "As you no doubt noticed, my brother-in-law is a drunkard!"

The word was harsh on her lips before she continued:

"One night when he was staying here Mama made certain that he was even more inebriated than usual. He was in fact carried to bed by the servants. When he came downstairs the next morning, Mama greeted him with a cry of delight and kissed him on both cheeks.

"My dear boy," she said, "you cannot imagine how happy you have made me!"

"The Duke looked absolutely astonished," Calista went on, "and Mama said archly:

" 'You were very naughty not to ask my permission first before you approached Ambrosine, but because she is so thrilled by your offer of marriage, I will forgive you!' "

"What did the Duke say?" the Earl

asked.

"What could he say? Mama was far too astute to speak to him alone. Ambrosine was in the room and so were a dozen other people who were staying with us. Obviously he could not remember anything about the night before, so I imagine that for the rest of his life he will wonder if he did or did not invite Ambrosine to be his wife."

"Is that really the truth?"

"You do not imagine my sister really wanted to marry such a creature? He had nothing whatever to recommend him except his title!"

Her voice was contemptuous. Then she continued:

"If you still question Mama's ingenuity, let me tell you about Beryl."

"That is your second sister?"

"We were christened alphabetically, A-B-C-D, the last is Deidre, who is only fourteen and still in the Schoolroom."

"Go on!" the Earl ordered.

"We all knew when the Marquis of Northaw came to stay that he was infatuated with a pretty married woman whom Mama had also invited."

"Why did she do that?" the Earl enquired.

"To make quite certain he did not cry off at the last moment."

"What happened?"

"It was quite obvious that the Marquis was not interested in Beryl, while she positively disliked him and made every excuse to avoid him. But Mama was too clever for her."

"What did your mother do?"

"She somehow contrived that the Marquis and my sister found themselves alone in the conservatory. Beryl told me later she was deliberately being very stiff and cold and talking in an uninterested fashion about the flowers, when Mama put her scheme into operation."

"What was that?"

"She let loose—I am never certain how she arranged it—two mice! They ran across the conservatory floor and Beryl, who has always been afraid of mice, screamed and clutched hold of the Marquis for protection!"

Calista made a little gesture.

"You can imagine the rest. Just at that particular moment, Mama *happened* to

113

come into the conservatory with several of her other guests."

"She put her arms round Beryl and kissed her, while the Marquis was congratulated by the men who had accompanied her. There was not a chance of his being able to escape or explain it was a misunderstanding."

"I must admit, if what you tell me is true, that your mother has a very ingenious mind," the Earl said.

"It is true! But I cannot find out what she has in store for you."

"You still believe that she really intends to force us together into marriage?"

There was still an obviously incredulous note in his voice even while he now admitted to himself that there must be some substance of truth in what Calista was relating.

"Mama said to me a month ago: 'It is time you were married, Calista, and I have chosen a husband for you.' "

"Did she say it without any preliminaries?"

"She has been telling me for some time that I must be married quickly," Calista answered. "You see I have been defrauded out of one year of my social life."

"What do you mean by that?" the Earl enquired.

"Well, immediately after Mama announced Beryl's engagement to the Marquis, his grandmother died and they could not be married for twelve months. So, as Mama refuses to have more than one daughter out at a time, I had to stay in the Schoolroom for an extra year. I am nineteen! Almost, as the French say, ready to *coiffer Sainte Catherine*!"

The Earl laughed.

"That is still very young, especially to me."

"Yes, of course," she answered. "You are nearly thirty. I looked you up in *Debrett*."

"You were telling me what your mother said," the Earl prompted.

"Mama merely said: 'I have chosen your husband and when you meet him, Calista, you will make yourself pleasant to him and not indulge in those tomboyish antics which would disgust any decent man.' "

The Earl laughed again.

"That was certainly plain speaking. I

115

cannot imagine that your mother would approve of your looking as you do now."

"Does it shock you that I am not wearing a skirt?" Calista asked. "It would be very difficult to climb a tree in one, and I find it easier to teach Centaur his tricks when I am dressed like this. Of course I keep well out of sight of Mama. She would have a heart attack if she saw me!"

"I am not surprised," the Earl said.

She gave a little gurgle of laughter.

"You are shocked! How amusing! I thought that with your reputation nothing I could do would surprise you!"

"My reputation?" the Earl enquired.

"People talk about you," Calista said simply, "and I am a very good listener. You are very much admired by men and women slobber about your attractions!"

She did not make it sound a compliment and the Earl remarked:

"I am not particularly interested in gossip. I want to know what your mother told you."

"Mama informed me there was no-one richer, more distinguished or more *persona grata* in society than the 'Elusive

Earl' of Helstone!''

" 'It is a challenge, Calista', she said, 'to destroy the legend that surrounds him. He will be your husband, and let me add that you are a very lucky girl.' "

Calista turned her eyes towards the lake.

"It was then," she said quietly, "that I decided to warn you."

"You do not wish to marry me?" the Earl enquired.

"Do you really think that any girl would wish to be married in such circumstances?" she asked. "And I have, as a matter of fact, decided that nothing and nobody will make me take the marriage vows unless I wish to do so."

"Meaning, I suppose that you must be in love?"

"Exactly!"

Her chin went up as she added in a defiant voice:

"I am sure it amuses you, as it would most of Mama's friends that I actually want to love my husband, and that he should love me."

"I have not said so," the Earl remarked.

"But you think it all the same," Calista

117

retorted. "I am well aware that the world would think I was tremendously fortunate to be your wife, however despicably you were tricked into marriage! But I have no intention of conforming to what is acceptable to other girls of my age, or indeed to Mama."

"You will have to marry sooner or later."

"When I do, it will be someone of my own choosing," Calista said sharply. "I expect you think that is impossible, but unless I find a man I can love with all my heart, then I swear I will remain single."

"Would your mother allow you to do that?"

"I will run away rather than acquiesce in her intrigues," Calista said passionately.

"That would not be easy," the Earl said quietly.

She was silent, and he thought that the silhouette of her profile against the silver water of the lake was very beautiful.

There would be many men, he knew, only too willing to lay their hearts at her feet and to love her in the way she wanted.

It seemed hard and almost cruel to be

sure—as he was sure—that her idealism would be overwhelmed by her mother's determination, and that sooner or later she would be married without her having any choice in the matter.

"I know what you are thinking," Calista said in a low voice. "But perhaps because I am older than Ambrosine and Beryl were at the time and perhaps too because I have much more brain than they have, I shall not be coerced or bullied as you think I will."

"I hope you are right," the Earl said. "At the same time I can see many difficulties and pitfalls ahead of you, especially if your mother behaves in the way that you have told me she does."

"Mama has a will of iron under that sweet and charming manner."

Calista spoke quite dispassionately as if she was discussing a stranger.

"I must thank you for warning me and for being so frank," the Earl said. "I will be honest with you, Calista, and say that, like you, I have no desire to be married. In fact I am determined to remain a bachelor."

"Then watch out for Mama!" Calista

warned him. "We must never be alone with each other—not for one second! I changed my place at dinner tonight. Mama will doubtless be very angry with me tomorrow, and we shall find ourselves together whether we like it or not."

"I would not like you to think me so ungallant that I am not prepared to say that I find you very interesting," the Earl said, "and you are certainly unpredictable!"

"I want to talk to you about your horses," Calista replied. "Why do you give them Greek names?"

"Like yours, which is Greek, I consider them more attractive than the usual ones under which horses are registered."

"I was thinking only last night when reading James Weatherby's *General Stud Book*," Calista said with a note of interest in her voice, "that I would hate to have a horse called Whalebone or Whiskers."

"Whalebone was described by his groom," the Earl said, "as 'the lowest and longest and most double-jointed horse, with the best legs and the worst feet I have ever seen in my life'."

Calista laughed.

"Nevertheless," the Earl continued, "both Whalebone and Whiskers were Derby winners."

"And Squirt is an even uglier name!" Calista said reflectively.

"The sire of Marske, who in turn sired Eclipse," the Earl remarked.

He saw the surprise in her eyes as she said:

"You know a lot about horses, do you not?"

"I hope I know a little about them."

"It is unusual," Calista said. "Most owners, at any rate the ones who come here, buy what is recommended, take their trainer's advice on which races they are entered and do not even bother to look up the breeding of the animals they have acquired."

"I think you are very scathing," the Earl said with a smile.

"I am trying to prove that Centaur is a descendant of Godolphin Arabian," Calista said. "I suppose you know who he was?"

"I do indeed," the Earl answered. "Godolphin Arabian, Darley Arabian and Byerley Turk were the Arab strain which was the foundation of all thorough-breds in this country."

"You really know what you are talking about," Calista said with a note of admiration in her voice which had not been there before.

"If Centaur is not an Arabian he may be a Barb," the Earl remarked.

He said this to see how much Calista really knew and if she was aware that the Barbs were the horses from North Africa, Libya, Tunisia, Algeria and Morocco and were second best to the Arabians.

"The Duke of Newcastle, when the Arabians came to England at the time of Charles II," Calista said, "loved Spanish horses and said that they were like Princes and Barbs like gentlemen of their kind!"

"He was undoubtedly right, as he was one of the greatest stud owners of the time."

Calista clasped her hands together.

"Oh, there is so much I want to ask you," she said, "so much I want you to tell me. It is too unfortunate that we cannot meet in the ordinary way, but it is impossible—quite impossible!"

"I still think you are over-dramatizing

your mother's power," the Earl said.

"I am not prepared to risk that I am mistaken—are you?" Calista enquired.

"I suppose not, and therefore I think we should return to the house. If by any chance we were discovered here, there would, I am sure, be no escape for either of us!"

"Would you really give in so tamely?" Calista asked and now the scorn was back in her voice.

"I would fight like an Arabian!" he answered. "But if one were lassoed expertly it might be hard to escape."

"Well, I have warned you. Your only safeguard is to keep with the other guests and not wander off by yourself. Do not speak to me if you can possibly help it."

"That is rather unfortunate, for I find talking to you, Calista, is a new and interesting experience."

"Only because I am a novelty," she retorted, "a tomboy unlike the other ladies to whom you condescend!"

The Earl raised his eyebrows.

"I do not think I care for that particular word."

"It is true, nevertheless!" Calista

declared. "If you heard some of the things the ladies say about you when they are gossiping after dinner, you would realize you are like a Sultan with a Harem competing for his favours."

"If you talk like that you will find quite a number of young men will be afraid of offering for your hand. A wife with a sharp tongue would be as difficult to control as a horse that bolts."

Calista laughed.

"I wish you could have seen your face when I fell off Centaur's back and you thought I was injured."

"It was a new experience to have a young woman literally throwing herself at my feet!" the Earl said dryly.

Calista laughed again.

"Even that stupid old groom who Mama insists must accompany me when I am riding in London could not believe that Centaur would throw me or that I could be thrown."

She gave a little sigh.

"I should have liked to show you some of the tricks Centaur can do. He really is fantastic, but for you to show any interest in him might seem to Mama to constitute an interest in me."

"I see there are fences higher than those in any steeplechase keeping us apart!" the Earl laughed.

"Do take it seriously!" Calista begged. "I knew when I first spoke to you that you would be inclined to treat the whole thing as a joke."

"You must admit it is a trifle far-fetched."

"You would find it much more far-fetched to wake up one morning and find you were married to me!"

"I admit that is an alarming thought," the Earl smiled.

"Then be careful!"

Calista rose from the seat under the honeysuckle as she spoke and looked out towards the lake.

She was very slim, and were it not for her small, exquisite features and huge dark eyes she might indeed have been the boy she was pretending to be in her masculine attire.

"Can you imagine," she said in a low voice, "what it would be like to come here with someone you loved? To watch the mists rising over the lake and believe they are the nymphs who live beneath the green waters; to feel the magic of the moonlight and know that the stars were wishes you had made for each other's happiness?"

There was something very soft and musical in her voice which had not been there before.

The Earl stood looking at her, and then he said quietly:

"I think what you have just described is what we would all want to find, but it eludes us."

Calista turned her eyes from the lake to look at him.

"So love is elusive—like you!"

"I am not particularly proud of that adjective," the Earl protested.

"I can understand that! Especially as it makes Mama determined she will prevent your remaining elusive any longer. What a trial importunate females must be in your life!"

She spoke mockingly and the Earl replied:

"Your mother is right in calling you a tomboy, Calista, but I should add that I find you a provocative little devil!"

"Thank you, My Lord!" Calista replied. "If I was wearing the right clothes I would drop you a curtsey. As it is, I had better lead the way as without a provocative little devil to guide you, you might get lost in the bushes!"

She went ahead so quickly that the Earl had some difficulty in keeping up with her. In a few minutes they had reached the house, and standing in the shadow of the rhododendrons he looked up at the magnolia tree.

"There is no need for you to go back that way," Calista said reading his thoughts. "I have a key to the garden-door and I will let you in. All you have to do is go straight upstairs and your bed-room is on the left."

She paused, then added:

"If by any unfortunate chance you did meet anyone, you went for a walk in the garden because you found it hard to sleep. No-one will ever suspect that you were not alone."

Without waiting for an answer Calista ran across the path to the house.

The Earl could see a door just a little to the right of his window.

Calista had drawn the key from the pocket of her pantaloons. She inserted it in the lock and opened the door for the Earl.

"Good-night!" she whispered almost beneath her breath.

"Good-night, Calista!" the Earl answered. "And may I thank you for a very unexpected and enjoyable discussion?"

She made a little grimace at him and he could see that her eyes were twinkling.

Then as he entered the house she shut the door behind him and he heard the key turn in the lock.

. . . .

The following morning the Earl found it difficult to believe his conversation with Calista had actually taken place, but there was little time for introspection.

He was called early and set off with Lord Yaxley to see the horses being exercised before the race, and to judge which of the magnificent animals assembled on Epsom Downs were likely to prove winners.

He found quite a number of his friends taking the same interest and there was no doubt that most of the other owners looked at the Earl's horses apprehensively and wondered whether there was any chance of beating them.

The Earl had runners in three races out of five, and there was in fact only one which he fancied he had little chance against—an exceptionally fine horse belonging to Lord Hillsborough.

Delos was of course being kept for the Derby the following day, and the Earl's trainer assured him that the horse was in excellent form.

When they returned to Chevington Court for breakfast and to change before returning to the racecourse, the Earl was not surprised to see no sign of Calista.

He did however hear Lady Chevington ask where she was.

"Miss Calista has already left, M'Lady. I thought Your Ladyship knew she was planning to arrive early on the course."

"Is she riding?" Lady Chevington asked.

"Yes, M'Lady."

"She knew quite well I wished her to

come in the carriage with me," Lady Chevington said sharply.

Then realizing it was too late for her to do anything about it she turned her attention to her guests, and there was no further mention of her daughter.

The Earl thought during the races that he had had a glimpse of Calista on the Downs on the other side of the course.

He was almost certain that he recognized Centaur's white star on his forehead and his two white front fetlocks.

But if it was Calista, she was keeping well out of sight of the stands, and he had the idea that she was more likely to watch the racing from the famous Tattenham Corner than from the more fashionable part of the course.

The Earl had a spectacular win in the second race and his horse won by a nose in the third.

His third entry, as he had expected, was beaten, but it was with a feeling of elation that he drove back to Chevington Court.

"You have had a good day, Osric?" Lord Yaxley asked.

"Excellent!" the Earl answered.

"I shall look forward to seeing you win the Derby tomorrow," Lord Yaxley went on.

"That is a different kettle of fish, as you well know," the Earl replied. "We shall be up against the finest horses in England and I am not entirely confident that Delos can stay the course."

"I think he will do it," Lord Yaxley said, "and I will tell you something else, Osric, it will be an exceedingly popular win. The crowd likes you and many of them put their money not only on the horse, but also on you!"

"You are being very kind to me all of a sudden," the Earl said with a cynical twist of his lips.

"I mean it, just the same," Lord Yaxley said. "There are a number of owners, as we both know, who do not mean a thing to the man who comes to the Derby for a bit of fun; but you are different."

.   .   .

The following day, as the horses swept round Tattenham Corner and bunched together started the long run down to the winning post, the Earl watched intently.

It was impossible at that distance to pick out his own horse amongst the brilliant kaleidoscope of red, green and yellow coats and as many different coloured caps.

The horses drew nearer and there was that strange expectant hush as if every man, woman and child held their breath.

Then right on the rails the Earl saw Delos moving ahead.

He was just a nose in front of the horse beside him, then a neck, then half a length, and a great cheer rang out as he passed the post two clear lengths ahead.

"Well done, Osric!" "Magnificent race!" "My congratulations, old boy!" "Bravo!"

Everyone seemed to be speaking to the Earl at the same time, and this time there was a glint of victory in his eyes and a smile on his lips as he went down the stand towards the unsaddling enclosure.

His trainer was so excited he was almost incoherent, and there were tears in the jockey's eyes when the Earl congratulated him.

Only Delos seemed supremely indifferent, tossing his head and seeming unfatigued after the long hard ride.

Back at Chevington Court his hostess and the rest of the guests showered the Earl with flattery and congratulations and as Lord Yaxley said afterwards, short of crowning him with laurel leaves, made it seem a Roman victory!

The pleasure of everyone was undoubtedly increased by the fact that the majority of them had backed Delos for substantial amounts.

It was not so much the Earl who had inspired them with confidence in Delos as Lord Yaxley who, having this time followed his friend's advice, wanted everyone else to be in at the kill.

"The bookmakers will not be feeling so happy tonight!" Lord Yaxley said to the Earl as they went up to dress for dinner.

"They will have done well yesterday," the Earl answered. "My second win was at 10—1."

"Are you running anything tomorrow?"

The Earl shook his head.

"I thought, if we were successful with Delos, my stable would be too over-excited to pay much attention to anything else.

There is always the Gold Cup at Ascot."

"You are never satisfied, Osric," Lord Yaxley teased.

Dinner was even more gay and entertaining than it had been the two previous nights. A number of other guests had been invited from nearby houses, and the Earl learnt there was to be dancing afterwards.

He wondered if this was a subtle way of inveigling Calista into his arms, but he had not been privileged to overhear a conversation which had taken place between Calista and Lady Chevington.

"You changed the places again last night at dinner, as well as the night before," Lady Chevington said severely. "You knew I intended you to sit next to the Earl."

"I am sorry, Mama," Calista answered, "but I was very anxious to be next to Lord George Bentinck, and I thought you would not mind my altering the cards."

"I minded very much," Lady Chevington snapped. "I had planned the table with the greatest care and, as you well know, I wish you to converse with the Earl."

"You cannot still have that ridiculous idea that I might marry him?" Calista enquired.

"It is not ridiculous and I have every intention that you shall do so," her mother replied.

"Then I promise you, you will be disappointed. I have no wish to marry the Earl and, as all the world knows, he has no interest in unfledged girls."

"In time young girls become married women, Calista, and that is what you will be."

"I doubt it, Mama, and certainly not with the Earl of Helstone."

Lady Chevington tightened her lips.

"You will make yourself pleasant to him, Calista, and you will dance with him this evening."

"I am sorry, Mama, but I think it very unlikely that I shall feel like dancing."

"What do you mean by that?"

"I have a sore throat. My nose is stopped up and I am afraid I am sickening for a cold."

"I do not believe a word of it!" Lady Chevington snapped. "You had better lie down before dinner. I want you to look your best."

"I hope I will not disappoint you, Mama," Calista said demurely.

Two hours later Lady Chevington was greeting her dinner guests in the Salon when the Butler came to her side.

"What is it?" she asked.

"Miss Calista has asked me to tell you, M'Lady, that she feels so ill and her cold is so bad that she is unable to dine downstairs this evening."

Just for a moment Lady Chevington was still, and her lips tightened in a hard line. Then as more people were announced she swept forward with a charming smile to exclaim:

"How nice of you to come! It is delightful to see you!"

4

The Earl had overheard what the Butler said to Lady Chevington and with a smile he thought to himself that Calista was being extra-cautious.

At the same time this meant he need not worry that evening about being detached from the other guests or finding himself unexpectedly alone with her in the Conservatory!

He therefore put the whole problem of Calista out of his mind and settled down to enjoy himself with his friends who wished to discuss the performance of every horse which had taken part in the Derby.

"You will now have to try for the Triple Crown, Osric," Lord Yaxley said and Lord George Bentinck agreed.

The Triple Crown meant that a horse won the 2,000 Guineas, the Derby and the St. Leger.

"I was thinking of running Delos at Ascot," the Earl said reflectively.

"You have two other horses in your stable which I shall certainly back if you enter them for the Gold Cup," Lord George remarked. "I should keep Delos for the St. Leger."

"Perhaps you are right," the Earl agreed, while another owner said somewhat sourly:

"Will no-one stop Helstone walking off with all the glittering baubles in one year? If he enters Delos, I shall certainly withdraw my animal."

The others laughed at him but he said:

"I am always prepared to bow to superior odds. God alone knows how Helstone always manages to produce better thoroughbreds than any of the rest of us can do."

"I think it is not only in the breeding," Lord George said, "but also in training. Helstone has his own methods which I have often thought are revolutionary, but they do produce results."

"Who can argue about that!" someone said crossly.

Once again the dinner was an epicurean delight and when the gentlemen joined the ladies in the Salon the Earl made his way to the card-tables, feeling disinclined to continue to flirt with the pretty Peeress who had sat next to him in the Dining-Room.

Tonight the ladies did not retire early because there was dancing and it was after midnight when finally everyone said good-night.

"I have enjoyed myself, Mama," the Earl heard the Duchess of Frampton say to Lady Chevington. "It is a pity Calista had a cold."

"It was very tiresome of her," Lady Chevington said with a note in her voice which was very different from the dulcet tones in which she had spoken to her guests.

"I expect she will be well enough to go racing tomorrow," the Duchess laughed. "You know Calista would never miss a race-meeting."

Lady Chevington did not answer. Then, collecting the lighted candles in their silver candlesticks which everyone carried on their way to bed, the party moved slowly up the staircase.

The Earl was almost one of the last since he had stepped back to tell the

Butler he would be leaving after the races the following afternoon.

He had decided that three nights at Chevington Court were enough, and he was sure that Calista would be glad when she saw the back of him.

At the foot of the stairs he found Lady Chevington talking with Lord George Bentinck and Lord Palmerston about the additions which had been made to the house down the ages.

"It is an amazing pot-pourri of different styles and periods," Lord Palmerston said.

"That is true," Lady Chevington agreed.

"What is so surprising is that each part seems to be the best of its own period," Lord George remarked. "Where we are standing now is the very finest George I while the Orangerie and the Library are perfect Queen Anne."

"I have deliberately kept their individual characteristics," Lady Chevington said, "and strangely enough, I find the Elizabethan Wing the most attractive. It still gives me a little pang when I think how much of the original house has been lost, but the Wing which remains is, in its way, quite flawless!"

"I am sure it is," Lord George remarked.

"I have furnished it with Tudor four-posters and when the panelling needs to be repaired I have to go on my knees to the Keeper of Ancient Churches to acquire the same linenfold pattern."

"Your taste is impeccable, dear lady!" Lord Palmerston said with an almost caressing note in his voice.

"How I would love a completely Tudor house," Lady Chevington said as she moved up the staircase. "There is a picture of this one as it was in 1560, when it was called 'Queen's Halt' because Elizabeth slept here. I must show it to you."

"I would like to see it," Lord George replied, "and you are lucky to have such an early painting."

"The house figures in the background of several conversation pictures," Lady Chevington told him, "but there is only one of the house by itself."

She turned as they reached the top of the stairs to say to the Earl:

"The picture we are speaking of hangs

in your bedroom, My Lord. I am sure you will not mind if I show it to Lord Palmerston and Lord George?"

"Of course not," the Earl replied.

They walked along the passage and he opened the door of his bedroom.

They were all four carrying candles which were unnecessary since there were two candelabra alight on either side of the four-poster bed and another with six candles standing on a table near the fireplace which illuminated the picture most successfully.

They walked into the room and the Earl lifting his eyes to the picture over the mantelshelf thought Lady Chevington was right in saying it was in fact an extremely interesting and unusual painting.

The great house with its brickwork red against the surrounding green of woods and parklands glowed like a jewel. Then as he drew nearer to the fireplace the Earl heard a sudden exclamation and turned round.

Lady Chevington and the two men with her were not looking at the picture but staring at the bed.

142

Incredulously the Earl saw Calista lying in the centre of it, her fair head spread out over the pillow and she was sound asleep!

For a moment no-one moved. Then in a voice of sharp indignation Lady Chevington ejaculated:

"Really, My Lord!"

For a moment the Earl could not think of a reply. Tactfully Lord George and Lord Palmerston moved towards the door.

The Earl was well aware there was a faint smile of amusement and perhaps of sympathy on Lord Palmerston's lips.

He himself had been involved in so many amatory adventures that he could not help having a fellow-feeling for another sinner.

Lady Chevington walked towards the bed and bending over put her hands on Calista's shoulders.

She shook her violently and as she did so the Earl realized that Calista must have been drugged.

She opened her eyes slowly as if her eyelids were heavy, and there was a bewildered look in them as she stared up at her mother's face not understanding where she was or what was happening.

"Wake up, Calista!"

Lady Chevington pulled her daughter roughly into a sitting position.

With an obvious effort Calista took her eyes from her mother's face and looked across the room to where the Earl stood watching.

"Where . . . am I? What is . . . happening?" she asked in a voice that was slurred.

"As if you did not know!" Lady Chevington replied. "I am deeply ashamed of you, Calista, but this is not the place nor the time to discuss your behaviour."

As she spoke she turned to pick up a dressing-gown which lay over an adjacent chair, and the Earl noticed that she did not have to look for it, being obviously aware where it was.

She pulled Calista from the bed and put the dressing-gown over her shoulders.

"You will now come upstairs with me."

She put her arm round her daughter as she spoke and drew her from the side of the bed towards the door.

The Earl stood without moving, watching them until as Calista passed him her eyes met his and he saw an expression of despair in them.

"I will talk to you, My Lord, in the morning," Lady Chevington said to the Earl as she reached the door, then she drew Calista from the room and the Earl was alone.

He stood for a moment staring after them, then sat down in an armchair, his lips set in a tight line.

He had to admit to himself that Calista had been right, completely and absolutely right, and he had been a fool to doubt her.

Why, he asked himself now, had he not accepted that she knew what she was talking about? Why had he not refused the invitation to Chevington Court as she had begged him to do?

It seemed incredible that he should have underestimated Lady Chevington's ingenuity and determination, especially after he had learnt how she had trapped the Duke and the Marquis into marriage with her other daughters.

He was well aware there was no honourable way now in which he could refuse to marry Calista.

The Earl was quite sure that neither Lord Palmerston nor Lord George would believe for a moment that he had not encouraged her into believing that she would be welcome in his bed.

His reputation with the fair sex would tell against him in any effort he might make to prove his innocence in the matter.

There was only one possible solution to the problem and that was to marry Calista.

If Lady Chevington had won, it meant also that she would not only have a wealthy and important son-in-law but also had won her wager of one thousand guineas and more important, had brought the 'Elusive Earl' to heel.

None, the Earl thought savagely to himself, would credit that the whole plot had been thought out and planned long before he arrived at Chevington Court.

Lady Chevington's sweetness, her capacity for making friends, her elaborate entertainments, the lavish amusements she provided for her guests made her very popular.

She might, as Lord Yaxley had said, be known to be ambitious, but it was obviously not even guessed to what extent she would have gone to make sure she got her own way and provided her daughters with the social position she considered essential to their happiness.

"Dammit!" the Earl said to himself. "There must be some way out!"

But he knew there was nothing he could do but accept the inevitability of it and take Calista as his wife.

'It might have been worse,' he thought.

Even as he raged inwardly at the thought of being trapped, he remembered that at least Calista was intelligent, at least she liked horses, at least she was very lovely.

At the same time, just as she had said she wanted to marry for love, so the Earl admitted now that was what he himself desired.

But if he was not permitted to find love, at least he would prefer to have a bride of his own choosing, not of Lady Chevington's.

He rose to his feet to walk up and down the room.

He had the feeling as he did so that the walls were closing in on him, the windows were barred, the door was locked, and he was a prisoner!

The prisoner of a woman who had been too clever for him, had outwitted him in the chase so that now there was no escape — none!

.   .   .

The following morning the Earl's first instinct was to leave the house before anyone was up and drive back to London. Then he told himself that would be the action of a coward.

He was well aware that if he was suffering Calista would be suffering too, and he could not forget the look of despair he had seen in her eyes when her mother had taken her from the bedroom last night.

'I must talk over the situation with her,' he thought. 'Perhaps she will find a solution which I cannot.'

He knew that Calista would want to defy her mother; to refuse to marry him. But she was under age!

Even if she had been twenty-one, parents had complete jurisdiction over their children and girls married whom they were told to marry, and there was no argument about it.

The Earl contemplated telling Lord Yaxley what had happened then thought the fewer people who knew of what had occurred, the easier it would be for Calista.

For it to become known that she had been found asleep in his bed, would be to bring down on her head the severest censure of the *Grandes Dames* of the social world.

There was also, the Earl knew, a large number of younger and more beautiful women who would be only too delighted to defame and pillory someone who had captured the 'Elusive Earl' as they had been unable to do.

He was quite certain that Lady Chevington would by this time have sworn Lord George Bentinck and Lord Palmerston to secrecy, and anyway they were gentlemen and would know they must be careful of what they said about a young girl.

"Pray Heaven it does not reach the ears of the Queen!" the Earl exclaimed.

Then he thought that if Her Majesty

was unaware of the amatory adventures of her Foreign Secretary, it was unlikely she would hear about Calista.

Lord Palmerston was known as 'Cupid' to his friends, but however keenly he might pursue a lovely woman he was a great gentleman and the Earl was certain that he could be trusted to say nothing which could harm Calista.

Lord George was slightly strait-laced and he would have been genuinely shocked at finding an unmarried woman in the Earl's bed.

Whatever he might guess happened where older and more sophisticated ladies were concerned, he would be surprised that the Earl who could evoke an ardent response from almost anyone he fancied, should choose a young and innocent girl.

It was with a hard look on his handsome face and a wary look in his eyes that the Earl went downstairs to the Breakfast Room.

It was usual at Chevington Court for the men to breakfast downstairs while most of the ladies ate in their own bedrooms.

The Earl was early, so there was only

Lord Yaxley together with a Politician and a prominent Patron of the Turf sitting at the table reading the sporting columns of the newspapers propped up in front of them.

"The papers speak of Delos in the most glowing terms, Osric," Lord Yaxley said as the Earl entered the room. "They hail him as another Eclipse, which should please you."

The Earl did not answer but went to inspect the long row of succulent dishes arranged on a side-table where several flunkeys awaited instructions once a choice had been made.

The Earl, having chosen what he required, sat down at the long table and the Butler asked him in a quiet voice whether he would drink tea, coffee or ale.

He chose coffee, noting that the other guests had chosen ale with the exception of the racehorse owner who was already drinking brandy.

"What do you fancy for the first race?" Lord Yaxley asked.

He was invariably somewhat talkative at breakfast, which other men often found irritating.

"I should think Lord Derby's horse is the best bet," the Earl answered, speaking for the first time.

"I thought you would say so," Lord Yaxley replied, "but some of the papers recommend an outsider called The Poacher."

"I saw him run at Doncaster," the racehorse owner interposed. "Personally I thought he had not much stamina, but he might manage to win over a short distance."

As Lord Yaxley prepared to argue the merits of other horses in the race, more guests arrived in the Dining-Room, among them Lord George and Lord Palmerston.

They both greeted the Earl heartily in a manner which he knew was meant to show him they had already put out of their minds the unfortunate episode that they had witnessed last night.

Lord Yaxley engaged Lord George in a long discussion as to the rights and wrongs of an accusation of 'bumping and boring' which had taken place in the last race yesterday and the Earl was able to concentrate on trying to read the newspaper he had in front of him and finish his breakfast in silence.

He drank a second cup of coffee and was about to rise to his feet when the Butler came to his side.

"Excuse me, M'Lord, but Her Ladyship would like a word with you in her Boudoir."

"I will come at once!" the Earl answered.

The Butler opened the door, then preceded him up the stairs and along a corridor which led to the part of the house where Lady Chevington had her private Suite.

As the went, the Earl was wondering whether he should accuse her of having deliberately engineered what had happened the night before. Then he told himself there would be nothing to gain by making a scene.

He was quite certain that Lady Chevington would deny having any knowledge of Calista's movements.

It would be all too easy for her to point out that she was expecting her downstairs to dinner and to take part in the dancing afterwards.

But when Calista had sent a message at the last moment to say that she felt too ill to appear, it was impossible for her, with a large number of guests in the house, even to contact her daughter until after everyone had left.

No, the Earl thought, there was nothing for it but to put a good face on what had happened and wait until he could talk over the situation with Calista.

The Butler opened the door and he was shown into Lady Chevington's Boudoir.

It was exactly as he might have expected it to be, fragrant with flowers, decorated with exquisite taste in the soft blue which was a becoming background for Her Ladyship's fair hair and pink and white complexion.

There was a delightful collection of French pictures on the walls, and one glance at the *objets-d'art* on the side-tables told the Earl that Lady Chevington had collected around her many treasures that any connoisseur would be proud to possess.

His hostess, wearing a morning-gown of flowing muslin interspersed with lace, was seated at her secretaire.

She rose as the Earl entered. Then after keeping silent until the Butler had closed the door behind him she said:

"I have sent for you, My Lord, because something very unfortunate has happened."

The Earl raised his eyebrows, but he did not reply.

"Calista has run away!"

This was not at all what the Earl had expected her to say, and he was genuinely taken aback.

"Run away?" he repeated. "Where to?"

"I have not the slightest idea," Lady Chevington answered, "but I learn that she left the house at dawn riding her horse Centaur."

"Do you think she may have gone to stay with friends?"

"I think it unlikely. I have in fact already sent a groom over to the house of the only girl in this neighbourhood with whom she has any intimacy, but I am almost certain the family are away from home. Anyway I do not think that Calista would ask them to help her."

"You think that help is what she is

seeking?" There was an innuendo in the Earl's tone.

"I wondered whether she had said anything to you which might give us an idea of where she would hide herself."

"You are admitting that she wished to hide?" the Earl said accusingly.

"I am admitting nothing!" Lady Chevington retorted. "I imagine the child is embarrassed after what happened last night, and I do not think she will be gone for long. In the meantime however I think it best for neither of us to say anything about it."

"I have nothing to say," the Earl remarked. "Shall we be frank with each other?"

"I see no reason for it," Lady Chevington replied looking at him straight in the eyes. "You will of course marry Calista, but the engagement cannot be announced until she is found."

"I am sure she was aware of that when she left home," the Earl said with a sarcastic note in his voice.

Lady Chevington walked across the room to the fireplace.

"I am not at all happy about this

156

situation," she said. "Where could Calista go? And how can she possibly look after herself and her horse?"

"I presume she had some money to take with her."

Lady Chevington shrugged her shoulders.

"I honestly do not know. Miss Ainsworth, my youngest daughter's Governess, informs me that she might have a few pounds, but she did not think she would have much more."

"A few pounds?" the Earl ejaculated. "That is ridiculous!"

"I think it is encouraging," Lady Chevington answered. "When Calista finds she cannot live on what little she has with her, she will come home. That is obvious, is it not?"

"I think you are showing little understanding," the Earl said sharply. "Have you any idea of the trouble in which a girl as attractive as Calista might find herself, travelling alone without protection and without money?"

There was anger in the Earl's expression which Lady Chevington did not miss.

"I am as perturbed as you appear to be,

My Lord," she answered. "At the same time, what can I do? I can inform the Police, if you think that is the wisest thing to do. But I think it would be in Calista's best interests to avoid a scandal."

She paused to add:

"As you are aware, the world will never believe for one moment that she has run away alone."

"She has run away from me," the Earl declared, "and from what you have planned for her so skilfully!"

"I see no point in our discussing anything but Calista's immediate predicament," Lady Chevington replied, blandly ignoring the suggestion which the Earl could no longer resist making. "We can only hope that after she has gone a few miles she will see reason and return here. In fact I am hoping we will find her back tonight after we return from the races."

"I intend to leave for London straight from the racecourse," the Earl said coldly. "My valet can leave in my travelling carriage as soon as the luggage is ready."

"If that is your wish," Lady Chevington agreed. "As I shall be in London tomorrow, I hope with Calista, we can arrange to meet and discuss on what date the announcement of your betrothal can be inserted in the *Gazette*."

"I expect to be at home all day."

The Earl bowed and went from the room before Lady Chevington could reply.

As he walked down the passage he thought he had detected an undeniable look of triumph in her large blue eyes, and it made him long to tell her exactly what he thought of her behaviour.

But the Earl was a very restrained person and he knew that to lose control of his temper would gain him nothing.

What was important was to see and talk to Calista, and as that was impossible then there was really nothing left for him to do except return to London as soon as possible.

The Earl spent a most unhappy day on the racecourse, finding it hard to concentrate on the horses, and finally leaving before the last race.

"I cannot think what is the matter with you, Osric," Lord Yaxley said not once but several times. "I have never known you in such a grim mood. You might have lost the Derby instead of winning it!"

The Earl did not enlighten him.

Instead he drove back in silence at a greater speed than usual, feeling that he needed the comfort and security of his own house.

More than once he told himself under his breath that he cursed the day he had ever entered Chevington Court.

It was not only he who must suffer, but Calista too; although he was quite certain that if Lady Chevington had not chosen him as her victim, it would have been somebody else equally unacceptable to her daughter.

But at least he personally would not have been involved.

He dropped Lord Yaxley, still trying vainly to find out what was worrying him, at his lodgings, then drove to Helstone House to find Mr. Grotham waiting for him with a large number of invitations, none of which he wished to accept.

He half-hoped, although he thought it unlikely, that Calista might have communicated with him. But amongst the private letters on his desk there was no handwriting like that on the note she had sent asking him to meet her on the bridge over the Serpentine.

'Where could she have gone?' he wondered.

It had in fact been puzzling him all day.

He had never contemplated what a girl could do when she ran away from home.

There were of course many young women who escaped from paternal authority by climbing out of their bedroom windows at night, but they always had someone to hold the ladder and to have ready and waiting a post-chaise in which they could speed away to Gretna Green.

But Calista was alone, with only Centaur as her companion.

He could imagine that with her beauty and with the outstanding appearance of her horse she would draw attention wherever she appeared, and anyone who saw her would think it strange that she was not accompanied.

The Earl wished he had talked with the grooms in Lady Chevington's stables before he left Epsom.

Then he told himself that they would have been unable to tell him any more than they had already told their employer.

If Calista had left at dawn, which the Earl knew was at about four o'clock in the morning, she would have had a good four hours' start before anyone was likely to discover she was not asleep in her bed.

Would she go North, South, East or West?

He was quite certain that she would not go to London. But because the thought of her worried him and at least he felt partly responsible, the Earl despatched a footman to Lady Chevington's mansion in Park Lane to find out if Miss Calista, or her horse, had turned up there during the evening.

The answer was that there had been no sign of her, but the Earl told himself that he was worrying himself unnecessarily. Surely after one night in some obscure village Inn or Posting House she had to come home to face the music?

His assumption was however far too optimistic, as he was to learn when Lady Chevington called on him at three o'clock the following afternoon.

It seemed to the Earl there was a definite suggestion of anxiety in her eyes and her first question after she had been announced was:

"Have you heard from Calista?"

"That was what I intended to ask you," the Earl replied.

Lady Chevington, extremely elegant in the latest fashion with a bonnet which framed her once beautiful face, sat down.

"Where do you think she has gone?" she asked.

"I have no idea," the Earl replied. "Has she friends that you had forgotten in some distant place such as Cornwall? She may have set out to put as much distance as possible between us both."

"I cannot think of anyone."

Lady Chevington was silent for a moment, then she added:

"I have always kept my daughters quietly in the School-room until they were old enough to make their début. I hate the half-grown, untidy adolescent stage when girls are always a bore. Calista had her Governesses, her tutors, her teachers, but she did not have many acquaintances or friends of her own age."

The Earl thought privately that that was why she had made a friend of her horse and spent so much time with him, and why also she was, as he suspected, unusually well read.

But he knew he must be careful not to show that he had had any contact with Calista of which her mother was not aware. So he kept silent as Lady Chevington continued:

"We have to find her! She must be somewhere quite near home, and surely people would have noticed her and her horse. Do you think we should employ a Bow Street Runner?"

The Earl considered this.

"I do know of a man who has retired, but who has a great knowledge of the countryside. Shall I have a talk with him?"

"I should be most obliged if you would do so," Lady Chevington answered, "and there is of course, no question of sparing any expense."

"Of course not," the Earl agreed.

They parted coldly, but the Earl had the idea that Lady Chevington was considerably more agitated and worried about Calista than she admitted. He wondered if in fact she had some idea that Calista would be likely to rebel against authority as her other two daughters had been unable to do.

The Earl sent for the ex-Bow Street Runner, only to find that he was crippled with arthritis in the hip and quite unemployable.

The Earl explained that Calista had run away from home and told him about the horse she was riding.

"Have you any idea, Robinson, where such a young lady would be likely to go?"

"Your Lordship says the 'orse be distinctive, M'Lord?" the man enquired.

"Not only distinctive!" the Earl replied. "Miss Chevington has taught him some unusual tricks. I saw some of them — he will come when he is called; keep just out of reach when somebody else tries to catch him; bow when he is told to do so! I am quite sure he has a whole repertoire he can display, if necessary."

"Then 'tis obvious, M'Lord," the ex-Bow Street Runner said, "that th' young lady, if her ran short o'money, would try to join a Circus."

"A Circus?" the Earl ejaculated in amazement.

"They are always alooking out for 'orses

like that, M'Lord, an' riders to display 'em."

"But how would she ever get in touch with a Circus?" the Earl questioned.

The ex-Bow Street Runner smiled.

"Ye travels too fast through the countryside, M'Lord, ye don't see what's goin' on, meanin' no disrespect! But there be circuses all over th' place at this time o' th' year. Some big, some small. Some so poor that it's 'ard on the animals, an' shouldn't be allowed. But wherever they sets up their tents there's always an audience, if only t' laugh at th' antics of th' clowns."

"I can understand that," the Earl said.

He remembered now noticing the tents and caravans of the Circus people as he had driven to Newmarket or to Epsom, but he simply could not imagine Calista associating with such vagabonds.

At the same time it was an idea!

"If her don't join in with 'em, M'Lord, 'ow would her be likely to live, if as ye say, her's got little money? Her might find some'un ter offer her a meal, but they mightn't be so keen about afeedin' th' horse!"

166

The idea of Calista being at the mercy of the type of man who with very ulterior motives, would talk to her because she was alone and offer to feed her, made the Earl angry.

"I am very grateful to you for your suggestions, Robinson," he said, "I am only sorry that I cannot expect you to go looking for this young lady."

"I can find Yer Lordship a young man who'd do th' sort of job I used t' do, if that's what ye require, M'Lord?"

"I will think about it," the Earl said, "and thank you, Robinson, for coming to see me."

A couple of sovereigns changed hands and the ex-Bow Street Runner hobbled away.

The Earl sat down at his desk.

A Circus was a ridiculous idea, he told himself, and yet what was the alternative?

Three days passed.

Lady Chevington called again and now her defences were down and she could not disguise that she was extremely worried.

"I have gone into every detail of Calista's disappearance," she said. "We have found that she was wearing her summer riding-habit, which is green, trimmed with white braid."

The Earl remembered that this was the outfit she had worn when he had first met her in the Park, but he did not say so.

"She has also taken with her two muslin dresses, very simple ones, the sort she wore in the morning at home and some underclothes. They were rolled up in a white shawl and tied to the back of her saddle."

She sighed.

"Of course my Head Groom was not on duty at that hour of the morning and Calista would not allow him to be woken. She roused one of the stable-boys to saddle Centaur and he was far too stupid to think of asking her where she was going, and can only remember that she thanked him and rode off."

Lady Chevington paused, and added:

"The maid who attends to Calista says that all she had in her purse was three sovereigns and a few pieces of silver, and she took none of her jewellery with her."

The Earl did not speak. After a moment Lady Chevington said pleadingly:

"We must find her. Although you may

not think so, I love my daughters and perhaps Calista the best. She is more like my husband than the others."

The Earl was about to make some harsh retort, thinking she had had a strange way of showing her affection. Then he saw there was an expression of suffering on Lady Chevington's face.

With unusual perceptiveness he realized that in pushing her daughters into such advantageous marriages she was thinking not only of her own social position, but of the position she would have liked to hold at their age.

She was trying to give them the sense of security and confidence that she had always lacked because she was not of the nobility.

It was wrong, but it was a contorted sense of love and had not sprung, the Earl decided, entirely from snobbery as he had thought at first.

"I see there is only one thing I can do," he said after a moment. "I must try personally to find Calista."

"Would you really do that, My Lord?" Lady Chevington asked. "I would indeed be very, very grateful."

It was quite an easy thing to say, the Earl thought, when Lady Chevington had left, but almost impossible to put into operation.

Where would he start to look for Calista? He really did not know.

However, because it gave him a sense of purpose and in some strange way a feeling of adventure, he cancelled his engagements.

Mounting the black stallion for which he had developed a liking, he set off the following morning to ride South, thinking vaguely he would look at what Circuses he encountered on the way.

It was a crisp morning with a touch of chill in the wind which was not to be expected in June.

The lack of heat made Orestes, the Greek name with which the Earl had rechristened the stallion, rather more skittish than usual, and they moved swiftly through the traffic and were soon out into the open country.

There the Earl took to the fields, regardless of the fact that he was trespassing, to gallop Orestes over the lush green land and take several high hedges in style.

He encountered his first Circus about midday, and it was the first of dozens, all of which the Earl was to find had something depressingly similar about them.

There was invariably one old and bored elephant and three or four mangy lions, usually too apathetic and toothless to be any sort of menace except in the imagination of small children.

There would be a tight-rope walker who balanced himself on a wire above the heads of the crowds and drew deep exclamations of horror as he swayed from side to side on the rope, balancing himself, apparently precariously, by sun-shades or a long pole.

The acrobats varied in skill although their tricks were always the same.

Some were young and agile, some were growing old and the mere act of swinging on a trapeze was quite an effort.

The better Circuses would have teams of horses either white or piebald; their manes and tails would be long and well-cared-for, and the Earl knew by the shine on their coats and the manner in which they moved that they were properly fed.

But in the smaller and poorer Circuses the horses were as inferior as the performers, and some seemed hardly capable of bearing the three men climbing on their backs and up onto each other's shoulders.

Some made the Earl feel that death would be a merciful release for them when it came.

But in every Circus the laughter and the gaiety depended on the clowns. Giants, dwarfs, deformations and freaks, there were always a half dozen of them, sometimes more, and they made the children shriek with laughter.

Older people also wiped the tears of merriment from their eyes as the clowns threw themselves about, tripped each other up, squirted water, ran round the ring holding onto the horses' tails or produced eggs from the noses of the children in the front seats.

After four days of wandering over the countryside and sleeping in whatever Inn he could find available when night fell, the Earl thought that he must be on the wrong track.

He could not visualize Calista with her loveliness and elegance in any of the

Circuses he had visited on the various village greens, any more that he could see Centaur amongst their ill-bred horses.

He thought that perhaps by this time she would have turned up again at Chevington Court or in London, and the sooner he returned home to find out if that was a fact, the better.

At the same time he could not help admitting to himself if he had not been worrying about Calista, he would have enjoyed himself the last few days.

He found a freedom he had never experienced before in being away from his servants and valets, the routine of his establishments and the companionship of his friends.

He could not remember when he had been alone for such a long time, but strangely enough he had never felt in better spirits.

He knew it was in part due to the simple food he was eating and the enormous amount of exercise he took.

He had the feeling as he rode Orestes over the fields that the stallion was enjoying himself as much as he was.

The horse might not look as well-groomed, and his saddle and bridle were not as well polished as they had been when they left London, but there was perhaps an exhilaration for both of them in feeling they had escaped from the conventional routine of their well-ordered lives.

All the same the Earl told himself he must go back.

Calista would have been found by now and he was quite certain that his staff and a great number of his friends, like Lord Yaxley would be anxious for his safety.

He rode back through Hertfordshire having made an extended circuit through the other Counties, taking Epsom as the pivot on which his search must revolve.

It was six o'clock in the evening when the Earl reached Potters Bar, a name he knew because there was a famous Horse Fair there once a year.

He reckoned that in an hour's time he would be in London. When he turned Orestes's head in the direction of the main highway he saw the tents of another Circus!

It was larger than those he had encountered in the last two days.

The 'Big Top' as the main tent was called, was in the centre of a field and round it were a number of other tents, caravans, and drays which conveyed the cages of the wild animals.

There was a performance taking place, and the Earl's first impulse was to ride on because it was getting late.

Then he told himself it would be worth while having a last look to refute the ex-Bow Street Runner's suggestion that Calista might have taken refuge in a Circus.

The Earl did not wish to leave Orestes too near to the big tent in case the children coming out after the performance should upset him.

The stallion had a habit of lashing out with a hind leg, and the Earl was aware that it would be dangerous to anyone approaching too near to him.

Seeing a small copse of trees at the end of the field the Earl rode towards it.

As he reached the shelter of the trees he realized that a small boy had followed him.

He was raggedly dressed but he looked honest, and the Earl asked:

"Will you hold my horse for me?"

The boy smiled eagerly.

"Aye, Guv. An' take good care o' 'im, Oi will!"

"Mind you do!" the Earl answered, "and I will give you a shilling when I come back."

The boy's eyes lit up with excitement.

"A shillin' guv? Ye did say—a shillin'?"

"A shilling if you keep with the horse and do not let anyone else interfere with him," the Earl replied. "Let him crop the grass, but keep your hand on his bridle."

"Oi'll do that, Guv."

The Earl dismounted and gave the bridle into the boy's hand.

Orestes had been ridden hard and the Earl was certain the devil had gone out of him.

He walked towards the Big Top. As he neared it he heard shouts and screams of laughter and knew that the clowns must be performing.

He suddenly felt tired and thought it was too much effort to watch yet another long-drawn-out performance of lions and acrobats, tight-rope walkers and indifferent horses.

He stood in the entrance looking into the tent and a voice said sharply:

"Sixpence th' best seats. Twopence an' a penny th' others."

"Have you any unusual turns?" the Earl enquired. "Or a horse that is outstanding?"

The man at the seat of custom was about to reply: "Ye pay ter find out," then he looked more closely at the Earl and changed his mind.

"We've some'at very special, Mister."

"What is that?" the Earl asked without much enthusiasm in his voice.

"Th' Masked Lidy an' Her Half-human Accomplice!"

The Earl was suddenly still.

"Her'll be on in a couple o'minutes, Mister."

The Earl put a shilling down on the desk in front of the man and forgot to ask for his change. Then he walked into the tent and took the nearest seat available.

The clowns were just running off, tripping over each other as they went, and following behind came a giant on stilts who was the obvious favourite of the children.

As they disappeared, the Ring Master, resplendent in red coat, white breeches, black hat and with a long whip in his hand, came into the arena.

"Ladies an' Gentlemen!" he began in a stentorian voice. "We've the great privilege and honour to offer you ternight a most unique an' amazing performance given by a lady of mystery with Her Accomplice who, although he looks like a horse, is in fact Half-human — Ladies an' Gentlemen — may I present — 'The Masked Lady an' Her Half-human Accomplice!"

There was a round of applause and Calista appeared.

She was wearing a red riding-habit spangled with stars and silver sequins. A black velvet mask edged with lace, Venetian fashion, almost completely obscured her face, but the Earl knew that he would have recognized her figure and the superb manner in which she rode wherever he might have seen her.

Centaur was also disguised. The white star had vanished from his nose and so had his white fetlocks. Instead he was all black, but his coat was shining and both his mane and tail had been meticulously groomed.

Calista took him first round the outside of the ring, then she showed off his tricks.

The Earl was fascinated by them, as were the audience who sat spellbound and in silence.

Centaur stood up on his hind legs, he knelt down and laid his nose against the floor, he danced, he did a dozen different tricks which Calista had taught him, all with a grace which reminded the Earl of the famous white Lipizzan stallions of the Spanish Riding School in Vienna.

As the applause rang out a cardboard coach came into the ring propelled by men walking inside it.

There was a coachman on the box and it was drawn by a small, rather miserable-looking pony.

Calista drew a pistol from her breast-pocket and held up the coach.

The men protested and while they were doing so Centaur seized in his teeth what purported to be a large bag of gold and carrying it away gave it to a poor old man at one side of the arena.

The children screamed and clapped

their hands together with joy. Then the men tumbled out of the coach pointing their guns at Calista and Centaur.

Calista rode Centaur to the side of the ring which was in fact very near to the Earl.

"Take it easy, boy!" he heard her say.

Then as the guns were all pointed at them the horse galloped across the ring, leapt spectacularly over the supposed coach and disappeared.

There was wild applause and Calista and Centaur reappeared, the horse bowing in the same way that he had bowed to the Earl near the Serpentine.

Right, left and centre he made obeisance. Then once again they vanished and the next turn appeared.

This was a Strong Man — swarthy, arrogant and muscular — in tights and spangled tunic, who the Earl knew from past experience would not only lift heavy weights but balance three, four and perhaps six people on his head and shoulders.

He waited until the performance had begun, then walked outside.

He had now to find Calista and, what was more important, persuade her to return with him.

He walked behind the Big Top to find, as he might have expected, the cages containing the wild animals — lions and tigers.

They looked rather younger and in better health than those he had seen at other Circuses.

There was a large number of horses, who had either just done their turn in the ring or else were preparing to do it.

In this Circus they were piebalds and with feathers on their head stalls and coloured bridles and saddles they looked impressive.

Nobody paid much attention to the Earl as he moved amongst the caravans, some of which were painted gypsy-fashion while others carried the name of the Circus boldly inscribed on them.

There were tents and the noise of voices, people hurrying about, men carrying props over towards the Big Top, dogs barking and a general hurly-burly of sound and movement.

The Earl walked on until at last he saw Calista.

She was talking to a number of women

who were gathered outside their caravans, some sitting on the steps, some on the grass, all of them dressed in brilliant colourful clothes.

Calista had taken off her hat and her mask but was still wearing the spectacular riding-habit which even at a distance the Earl could see looked cheap and tawdry outside the tent.

The women were laughing at something she said, and the Earl moved away.

He had no desire to confront Calista in front of other people and perhaps upset her.

Keeping out of her view he watched, and presently he saw her walk from the group of women and go towards a small painted caravan which was a little apart from the others, in fact on the outside of the whole encampment.

He followed her and saw that Centaur was waiting for her.

"I will change first," he heard Calista say as she reached the caravan.

As if the horse understood he waited at the steps merely swishing his tail because the flies bothered him.

The Earl also waited, keeping his eyes

on the caravan but not drawing too near until it would be easy to speak to Calista alone.

She came out to the top of the steps wearing what seemed to him to be a long gypsy skirt of bright red and a white blouse with a shawl over her shoulders.

Then just as the Earl was about to go towards her another man appeared, a thin, tall man wearing the clothes of a Clown, his face white, his mouth a gash of crimson.

"Shall I unsaddle Centaur for you, *Chère*?"

He spoke with a broken accent and the Earl was certain he was French.

"Thank you, Coco," Calista replied, "but you must not be late for your entrance."

"I come on after Manzani," the Clown replied, "and we know, *hélas*! we know how long he takes over his bows."

Calista laughed.

"He enjoys the applause!"

"He is greedy — *Qui*?" the Clown remarked.

Calista laughed again.

"We all like to be appreciated."

"You, *Chère*, were *merveilleuse ce soir!*" the Clown said.

"Thank you, Coco," Calista replied.

The Clown had taken off Centaur's saddle and he put it just inside the caravan door.

Calista removed the bridle and centaur, with a buck to show there was still some spirit in him, moved away to where the grass was sweeter.

There were sounds of tumultuous applause coming from the tent.

"You had better go, Coco," Calista said urgently.

As if the Clown realized he had cut it fine, he turned and ran through the tents and caravans holding onto his tall hat as he went.

A moment later, just as once again the Earl was about to walk forward to Calista another man appeared.

He wore a long red cloak over his spangled trunks and the Earl immediately recognized him as the Strong Man whom he had seen entering the ring.

He was in fact a commanding figure as he moved towards Calista.

"You must have been a great success,

Manzani," Calista said. "I could hear the applause."

"We are both successful," Manzani replied.

He spoke English with a slight accent in a deep, rather boastful voice which the Earl found irritating.

"I want to talk to you."

Calista shook her head.

"I have to rest. Have you forgotten we are moving on later this evening? We will be awake all night."

"I'll help you."

"I can manage, thank you."

"I want to help you — you know I always want to help you."

"You are very kind," Calista said, "but I can manage quite well by myself."

"No woman can manage by herself," Manzani said. "Together we make a good team. Soon we'll leave this poor Circus and join one of the big ones. They'll welcome us and we'll be rich — very rich!"

"It is very kind of you, Manzani," Calista said, "but I prefer to work on my own."

"And that is something I can't allow

185

you to do."

While they were talking the Earl, keeping concealed behind the other caravans, was drawing nearer.

Now he could hear every word they said to each other, and he could see too the uncertainty in Calista's face.

"You'll come with me," the Strong Man said putting out his arms. "You'll be my woman and we'll be 'appy — very 'appy — together."

"No!" Calista said.

She would have moved backwards into the shelter of her caravan but Manzani put out his bare arms and took hold of her.

He pulled her against him and she gave a little cry.

The Earl strode purposefully towards them.

"Stop!" he said commandingly. "Leave that lady alone!"

5

For a moment both Calista and Manzani were surprised into silence. Then, as the Strong Man turned round to face the Earl, Calista said in a low voice:

"How did you find me?"

The Earl did not answer the question; but walking up to her, he said quietly:

"I have come to take you home, Calista."

Manzani suddenly moved in front of the Earl.

"Get out of here!" he shouted. "You can see you're not wanted!"

"I have a prior claim on this lady," the Earl said firmly.

"That remains to be seen!" Manzani retorted.

As he spoke he struck out without warning at the Earl, who only just managed to avoid Manzani's fist striking him in the face by stepping backwards.

The blow caught him on the shoulder,

making him stagger. Then almost before the Earl could regain his balance Manzani struck at him again.

This time the Earl was ready and parried the blow. They were now fighting in earnest, Manzani with a violence and total disregard for fair fighting which was in itself frightening.

He was stronger, heavier and with a greater length of arm than the Earl, who was further handicapped by the fact that he was wearing Hessian boots which slipped on the damp grass and a tightly fitting whipcord coat which restricted him.

However he caught Manzani a sharp blow on the side of the face which made the foreigner lose his temper.

Those of the Circus knew that the Strong Man was easily aroused to anger and was a bully to all those who worked for him.

There was now an ugly expression on his face as he rushed at the Earl and grabbing him round the body with both arms tried to squeeze the breath out of him.

It was a bear-hug from a man who was used to exerting his over-developed muscles to their greatest strength, and for a moment the Earl felt he was unable to breathe and that his ribs were cracking under the strain.

Then he fought himself free, but as he did so his foot slipped and Manzani caught him a terrific punch in the face with his right hand, followed by his left on the point of the chin.

The Earl fell backwards onto the ground.

Calista gave a little cry of sheer horror! Then as the Earl lay unconscious she saw that Manzani was bending over him intending in his anger to hit him again and again in the face and chest.

Even as the Strong Man drew back his arm to smite his prostrate rival he received a blow on the back of the head which made him fall forwards followed by another which laid him out face downwards on the grass.

Calista threw down the iron tent-peg with which she had hit Manzani and knelt beside the Earl.

His eyes were closed and there was a trickle of blood running down his chin.

She looked at him helplessly until she

heard a familiar voice say:

"What has happened, *Chère*?"

She looked up and her voice had a little sob in it as she replied:

"Help me — please help me, Coco."

"Who is he?"

There was only a moment's pause before Calista replied:

"My husband!"

"*Votre mari*? Manzani'll kill him when he recovers!"

"Yes, I know," Calista agreed. "We must get him away."

She wiped the blood from the Earl's chin with her handkerchief, then rose to her feet to say urgently:

"His horse will be tethered somewhere near. Please find it, Coco."

The Clown pulled his tall hat from his head and wiping the greasepaint from his face with the sleeve of his costume he hurried off.

Calista gave a low whistle and in a moment Centaur came trotting to her side.

She picked up his bridle from the floor of the caravan, and having put it on she lifted the saddle onto his back and fast-

190

ened the girths.

Then with a quick look at the two prostrate men she went into the caravan to bundle everything she possessed into the white shawl in which she had brought her things from Chevington Court.

There was no time to roll them neatly and tie them on the back of the saddle. Instead she knotted the four corners of the shawl together and leant out of the caravan to hitch it onto the pommel.

There being no sign yet of Coco she went inside again to change with trembling hands into the green riding-habit that she had worn when she left home.

She was just dressed and holding her hat with its long veil in her hand, when she heard Coco's voice and came from the caravan to find him coming towards her accompanied by a small, ragged boy who was leading the Earl's stallion.

The Clown saw that Centaur was saddled and that Calista was dressed in riding clothes.

"*Hélas*! You are leaving with him?" he asked.

"I must, Coco," Calista replied, "but I cannot do so without your help. He is not capable of riding."

She saw the Frenchman's lips tighten. Then while his eyes pleaded with her he said quietly:

"You know I will do whatever you want me to do."

She gave him a faint and worried little smile, then turned to the ragged boy.

"Is there a comfortable Inn anywhere near here?" she asked.

"Th' Guv there," the boy said pointing to the Earl, "promised me a shillin' to mind 'is 'orse."

"I will give you two shillings," Calista replied, "if you will lead us to an Inn."

"Two bob?" the boy ejaculated. "Thank ye, Missus. There be th' 'Dog and Duck' in th' village."

Calista remembered seeing the very unprepossessing Inn as they had come through Potters Bar.

"Is there no other nearby?" she enquired.

"There be th' Postin' Inn," the boy replied, " 'tis about half o'mile from 'ere on the main 'ighway."

"That is where we will go," Calista decided.

She turned to Coco.

"We have to get m . . my . . husband into the saddle and you must ride behind him and hold him steady."

For a moment she thought he would refuse, then with the greatest difficulty and by all three of them, including the small boy, exerting their utmost strength they managed to lift the Earl from the ground and into the saddle of the stallion.

Fortunately Orestes was more concerned with cropping the grass than fidgeting or refusing to be mounted, as he might have done earlier in the day.

Somehow they got the Earl astride the horse, and as Calista had suggested, Coco mounted behind him and held him in his arms.

It was a question of balance more than anything else, but the Clown, Calista knew, was himself a good rider and often doubled his part in the ring by riding one of the show-horses if they were short handed.

At last they were ready to move off and Calista knew by the sound of applause from the Big Top and the music being played noisily by the Brass Band that the performance was coming to an end.

"We must go!" she said urgently.

Pulling at the stallion's bridle the boy led the way across the field while Calista, on Centaur, followed behind.

She was desperately afraid that someone would see them go and try to prevent them from leaving, or at least enquire what had happened to Manzani.

He was lying just where he had fallen, his red cloak spread over his body so that it was a vivid patch of colour, which anyone might notice and go to investigate.

But they were fortunate, for almost the entire company of the Circus, having taken their final bow, were concerned only with leaving the Big Top with the horses and there was the usual *mêlée* and commotion amongst the tents and caravans.

At the other end of the tent the audience was pouring out; small boys shouting, screaming and imitating the clowns, their elders now that the entertainment was finished, in a hurry to return to their homes.

At the end of the field Calista saw a high hedge which would screen them from curious eyes and as they reached it she looked back and thought that a strange and yet interesting chapter of her life was finished.

It was just by chance that she had come upon the Great Carmo's Circus in a field on the outskirts of Guildford the day she had left home.

She had already covered twelve or fifteen miles and she was looking for an Inn where she could water Centaur and get herself something to eat.

She had, however, been arrested by the sight of the pie-bald horses being exercised in the field while a big tent was being erected.

They were following each other round and round an imaginary ring and she realized that they were well-trained.

She watched attentively the manner in which they turned at the word of command or at the crack of the whip.

The Riding Master, who as it happened was also the owner of the circus, noticed Calista, as was to be expected, and went to speak to her. He admired Centaur and enquired if she would like to see the afternoon performance.

She questioned him as to how he trained his horses.

Because he answered her questions and she found it so interesting she showed him some of the tricks she had taught Centaur, including the way he would dance on his hind legs when she asked him to do so.

"Who are you, lady?" the Ring Master asked when he had congratulated her on Centaur's skill, "and where're you going?"

"I am nobody of any importance," Calista answered, "and at the moment I am going nowhere."

He did not question her further and she learnt later that the Circus people never showed their curiosity or asked inquisitive questions of each other.

"In which case why do you not join us?" the Ring Master enquired.

For a moment Calista felt he must be joking. Then when she realized he was serious she saw that it could be a temporary solution to her problems.

She did not think that her mother, or the Earl, if he were interested, would expect to find her in a Circus, and she was well aware that her appearance and that of Centaur would excite comment if they stayed alone at Inns, however isolated.

There was another difficulty which she had only really begun to consider when she was already some distance from her home.

She had not enough money with her!

She was so used to being looked after by governesses, secretaries, servants of all descriptions, and her mother that she had never paid for herself anywhere.

She had therefore not realized when she had run away so impetuously in shame of what had happened the night before, that she would require a great deal more money than she had with her to keep herself and Centaur from going hungry.

She thought as she rode further and further away from Epsom that she should have at least brought her jewellery with her which she could have sold. But she had been so anxious to disappear and not to have to face the Earl after what had occurred, that she knew now that she had been incredibly and lamentably stupid.

The suggestion of the Ring Master, who she was to learn was always referred to as 'The Boss', was a solution to her difficulties, and after she had met the other members of the Circus she had begun to enjoy the unusualness of her new life.

She had of course not calculated the effect she would have on them as a woman and a very pretty one at that.

Coco fell in love with her as soon as they met, and she was grateful for his devotion and the way he would help her groom Centaur and park her caravan where she liked it to be, away from the noise and chattering of the other women.

But Manzani was a very different problem, he was a fiery mixture of Czech and Turk, although he called himself by an Italian name because he thought it sounded more romantic.

He was an emotional, jealous and somewhat cruel man, who frightened Calista.

She tried to avoid him but it was not easy, and more than once she had thought she would have to ask the Boss himself to tell Manzani to leave her alone.

It was most unfortunate, she thought now, that the Earl should have appeared just when Manzani had declared his intentions more positively than ever before.

She wondered desperately as she followed the stallion across the next two fields whether the Earl would ever forgive her for involving him in such an unpleasant and humiliating situation.

She was quite certain that he was in fact a very experienced pugilist, but no match for a man like Manzani who had been fighting crudely and primitively in brawls all his life.

She had been well aware also that the Earl was severely hampered by the clothes he wore and his Hessian boots.

Even so, she knew that his pride would resent the fact that he had been defeated by a Circus performer and had not been able, however bravely he had tried, to defend her from Manzani's unwelcome advances.

There was nothing she could do at the moment, Calista thought, except try to nurse the Earl back to health.

She could only hope that he was not dangerously injured by Manzani's superior strength, although she knew how powerful his bear-hug could be.

Only a few nights ago she had seen him half-kill a drunken soldier who had drifted into the Big Top with several companions and had jeered and mocked at each turn.

They had laughed at Manzani's appearance and belittled his strength in loud, drunken voices.

Manzani had waited outside.

He had taken them all on, three had fled, or rather staggered away as quickly as possible, but the fourth had stood his ground and Manzani had smashed into him to leave him unconscious and bleeding in a ditch.

The Posting Inn came into sight and Calista rode forward saying:

"I will go ahead and make arrangements, so that they will be ready for you."

She did not wait for Coco's reply but trotted Centaur into the yard of the Inn, and as the ostler came forward she said in an authoritative voice:

"I wish to see the Landlord immediately!"

He must however have seen her through the window, for by the time she had dismounted he was at the door bowing.

Calista had put on her hat with the

floating gauze veil as they came across the field, and although she looked slightly dishevelled there was no doubt that her elegant habit and the fine breeding of Centaur commanded respect.

"Are you the Landlord?" she asked.

"I am, Ma'am; it'll be an honour to accommodate you."

"I am not alone," Calista said. "My husband and I were assaulted by footpads as we were on our way to London. He fought them most bravely but would have been killed had we not been rescued by some passing Circus folk. One of those who assisted us is bringing my husband here now, and I should be glad if you would prepare your best bedroom and send immediately for a Doctor."

"Of course, Ma'am, of course!" the Innkeeper bowed. "Those footpads are notorious round here. They terrorize the neighbourhood and should be hunted down by the military. But we'll do everything in our power to help you and your good man."

"Thank you!" Calista said with dignity.

As she spoke the stallion was led into the yard and the landlord could see the

Earl supported in the saddle by Coco.

Despite the fact that more blood was now covering his chin, that his head was sagging forward and one eye was closed from the blow in the face that Manzani had given him, he still looked distinguished and was obviously a Gentleman of Quality.

The Landlord called for a potman and a porter, who lifted the Earl down from the horse and carried him into the Inn.

Coco dismounted and Calista gave instructions to the ostlers to take both horses into the stables and see that once they were unsaddled they were fed and watered.

Opening her purse she took out a florin for the small boy.

"Will you promise me," she said before she gave it to him, "that you will not speak to anyone of what you saw at the Circus, or where we can be found?"

"Cross me 'eart, lidy," the boy answered, his eyes looking greedily at the florin.

She gave it into his hand and he rushed away as if half-afraid she would want it back.

Calista held out her hand to Coco.

"Thank you, Coco," she said quietly.

"Shall I never see you again, *Chère*?" he asked, and she saw the pain in his eyes.

"I shall think of you and always be grateful," she answered.

He gave a sigh of despair as if he realized that to protest would be hopeless. Then he raised her hand to his lips.

"I shall hope that this is not the end," he said. "*Au revoir*."

"*Au revoir*, Coco," Calista said, "I shall always remember you as a true and kind friend."

She turned away because she could not bear the unhappiness in his face and went into the Inn without looking back.

The Landlord with the other men had carried the Earl upstairs and were undressing him on a big bed in a low-ceilinged, raftered room which was not unattractive.

There was a bow-window overlooking a garden at the back of the Inn, and beyond it was an uninterrupted view of fields and woods stretching away into the distance.

"I've sent for the Doctor, Ma'am,"

203

Calista heard a woman's voice say, and she found a buxom country-woman dipping her a curtsey, whom she supposed to be the Landlord's wife.

The woman carried Calista's white shawl in one hand and a roll which she guessed must have come from the back of Orestes' saddle and would contain everything the Earl had brought with him as requisite for his journey.

"It's real sorry I am, Ma'am to hear about your husband," the Innkeeper's wife said in a voice full of sympathy. "Those footpads ought to be hanged — that's what they deserve!"

"They do indeed!" Calista agreed. "We are fortunate to have escaped from them with our lives."

As she spoke she saw the Landlady's eyes rest for a moment on her gloveless hand and added quickly:

"They took all my jewellery, including my wedding-ring, but my husband started to fight them before they could take his purse."

She thought the Innkeeper would be relieved to think he would be paid, and she was sure the Earl would not have been as stupid as she had been and would have set off on his journey with adequate funds.

"It's disgraceful — that's what it is!" the Innkeeper's wife exclaimed, "and a wedding-ring is what every woman, Ma'am, high or low, treasures and can never be replaced."

"That is true," Calista said with a little sigh. She looked back over her shoulder to see that the Earl was now between the sheets, then she said:

"I wonder if you have a room near this one where I can sleep? I am sure my husband should be kept very quiet and not be disturbed, but of course I wish to be close enough to nurse him."

"I quite understand, Ma'am," the Innkeeper's wife said. "There's actually a small dressing-room communicating with this chamber. It is what the gentlemen usually occupy, but perhaps you will find it convenient until your husband is better."

She opened a door as she spoke and Calista saw a bedroom which was a great deal bigger than the caravan in which she had been sleeping, and she assured the Innkeeper's wife that it would suit her perfectly.

Seeing the woman looking curiously at the white shawl she said:

"The thieves scattered everything I had with me about the roadway. I only hope I have left nothing essential behind, but I should be grateful if my two gowns could be pressed and I am sure you have a valet who will look after my husband's things properly?"

She was assured that the Inn could provide every possible service.

Then as the Landlord was about to leave the Earl's room Calista thanked him.

"May I know your name, Ma'am?" he asked.

"Yes, of course," Calista answered. "It is Helstone. Mr. and Mrs. Helstone. My husband and I live in London."

"The Doctor should be here soon, Ma'am, and I am thinking that, after he's been, you'd be ready for a bite of supper!"

"I should indeed!" Calista agreed.

The men who had carried the Earl upstairs went from the room with the exception of the valet, a small, thin, wiry little man who assured Calista that he would be within call should she need him at any time.

At last Calista closed the door behind him to go to the bed and look down at the Earl.

During the ride across the fields his eye had swollen to frightening proportions, but she knew that it was not such a deadly injury as had been inflicted on his chest.

It was however difficult to ascertain how badly he had been hurt until the Doctor had examined him. So she went into the next room to take off her riding-hat and tidy her hair.

Then she returned to sit by the Earl's bed, her eyes on his face.

It seemed to be fated, she thought, that they could not avoid each other.

She had done her best to warn him not to come into her life, and yet he had insisted; and now after she had run away to save him and herself he had appeared again and there was nothing she could do but nurse him back to health.

She knew she could not just send for his carriage and his servants and humiliate him by allowing them to see him in his present condition.

She knew too there would be too much explaining to do, even if she just disappeared again.

So the only way that she could make reparation for what was in fact wholly her mother's fault was to keep what had occurred a secret from everybody.

The Doctor arrived quicker than she had expected.

He proved to be a bluff, hard-hunting country physician, who was used to dealing with riding accidents and seemed to have a considerable knowledge of bones.

He examined the Earl.

"I would not mind wagering quite a considerable sum, Mrs. Helstone, that your husband, who is a fine specimen of a young man, has nothing much wrong with him, except perhaps for a cracked rib or two! I'll strap him up. He'll be uncomfortable for a short time, but he'll not come to any permanent harm."

"I am glad about that!" Calista said. "And you do not think his jaw is broken?"

The Doctor smiled.

"He's going to have a black eye that will spoil his attractions," he said, "and he's not going to feel like laughing for a few days! But he's lucky that those damned footpads, if you'll forgive my language, didn't break his nose!"

"His nose?" Calista asked.

"The last man they attacked had his nose badly broken and had an arm in splints for six weeks!"

He strapped the Earl tightly round his chest, told Calista to put goose-grease on his bruises and promised to look in the following day.

"How long will he be unconscious?" she asked.

The Doctor shrugged his shoulders.

"He'll feel pretty sorry for himself when he does come round!" he warned her. "So the longer he knows nothing about it, the better! I'll leave you a little laudanum in case he is restless in the night. It'll do him no harm and he's going to feel uncomfortable strapped up like a trussed gamebird!"

He laughed at his own joke, gave Calista a small bottle of laudanum and went downstairs where she could hear him chattering with the Landlord before he left the Inn.

She changed from her riding-habit into

209

one of her simple muslin gowns that had been pressed for her and went downstairs to eat alone in the private parlour.

The valet sat by the Earl while she was away, and when she returned after dinner he informed her that there was no change in the patient's condition.

Calista ordered some lemonade in case the Earl should wake and feel thirsty in the night. Then because it had been a long day and she was in fact very tired, she undressed in the small adjoining room and got ready for bed.

She had fortunately brought with her from home a light cotton wrapper that she could wear over her thin muslin night-gown. She had it on and was brushing her hair in front of the mirror when she heard a slight sound.

She ran into the next room to find the Earl groaning and trying to turn from side to side.

She bent over him to feel his forehead and realized there was no fever.

She was however certain that the pain his chest must be suffering from the cruel bear-hug he had received at Manzani's hands was beginning to percolate through to his mind.

Sure enough a few minute's later the one eye he could open flickered and he looked directly at her.

"You are all right!" she said quietly. "You have been hurt, but you are all right!"

As if her voice was reassuring he closed his eye again, but a few minutes later he said with difficulty:

"Where — am — I?"

"We are at an Inn," Calista replied. "Are you thirsty?"

He made a sound which she interpreted as saying he was and she lifted the glass of lemonade to his lips, supporting his head with her other arm.

She realized it was very painful for him to move his jaw and also his lip was cracked where it had been bleeding.

After a few sips he required no more, and she laid him back very gently against the pillows.

He looked at her and she was not certain whether he was thinking over what she had said or was in fact too bemused to understand anything in his half-conscious state.

After a little while he went to sleep.

.   .   .

The Earl opened his eyes and realized that he must have been asleep for a long time. In fact he thought he must have done a great deal of sleeping these last two days.

He was still in pain: when he moved it caused agonizing pain in his chest and he still found it hard to speak.

Nevertheless he knew he was better, even though the pain of the last two days had been almost unbearable.

His eye in particular was very sore.

He had seen in the mirror, when the valet shaved him, the blue and orange bruise which covered half his cheek and shaded to purple round the eye. It gave him a most fearsome appearance.

But now as he stirred, Calista rose from the window-seat where she had been sitting looking out into the garden and came to his side.

"Are you feeling better?" she asked in a soft voice. "You have slept since noon and it is now four o'clock in the afternoon."

She knew it was hard for him to speak, so she talked to him.

For two days their means of communication had been sparse. Calista used to ask the Earl if he wanted a drink; whether he felt he could eat anything; whether the pain was better. He replied with a nod or a shake of the head.

However, the Doctor, who had called this morning, was well pleased with him.

"Your husband was in splendid physical condition," he told Calista, "and that's what really counts when a man has been savagely knocked about. Do not worry about him, Mrs. Helstone. He will be on his feet again in a week."

Calista could not help wondering what the Earl would think about being confined for another week!

She suspected that the fracture of his ribs had been rather worse than the Doctor had thought at first, and she knew from experience of riding accidents that it was dangerous for anyone who had suffered such injuries to do too much too soon.

Now she sat down on the side of the bed and smiled at him.

"You are getting better," she said. "But I know it still hurts you to speak, so let me talk to you."

She thought the expression in the Earl's eyes was encouraging and she said:

"You must hurry up and get well. I have so much to tell you, and something very exciting!"

She realized the Earl was interested and she continued:

"When I was with the Circus there was a Frenchman — one of the Clowns — who had some books that he had brought with him from France. In one of them there was the story of Godolphin Arabian."

She paused and asked:

"Are you too tired for me to tell you about it?"

The Earl shook his head just perceptibly.

"When I read it," Calista went on, "I was so afraid that I would never see you again to tell you. You may know some of the tale, but it was all new to me."

The Earl was watching the expression on her face as she said:

"Godolphin Arabian was originally called Scham, an Arab horse which was given to King Louis XV by the Bey of Tunis in 1731. With him, along with seven other Arabs which were part of the gift, went a slave called Agba who had looked after him since he was a foal, and who was in fact deaf and dumb."

Calista's eyes were shining and her voice was filled with excitement as she told the Earl how the French King was not only an indifferent horseman but also a cowardly one, and Scham was a very spirited, fiery animal.

The King gave orders to his Master of Horse to dispose of all his Arabians, and Scham and Agba fell into the hands of a wood-carter.

Calista's tone deepened as she related how the carter turned out to be the most despicable brute in the City of Paris, a man of unspeakable cruelty, so that both Agba and Scham had to struggle for their lives day and night.

They were put on starvation rations and beaten continually, and their only solace in the misery that they suffered was when they were befriended by a small cat which Scham liked and licked with the tip of his tongue. After that the two animals became inseparable.

"Then their luck changed," Calista continued. "In January the following year, when the streets of the Rue Dauphine in Paris were slippery with ice, a crowd had gathered to watch while a carter unmercifully beat and kicked the fallen body of a horse."

There was a throb in her voice as she went on:

"He had gone down between the shafts with a load of wood that was too heavy for him.

"By chance a Mr. Edward Coke, an Englishman happened to be passing. He saw the tormented, blood-stained body of the horse and a small, brown-skinned man stretched protectively across the animal to save him from the blows.

"Mr. Coke, who was a Quaker, bought the horse as a good deed and an expression of his thanks to God for the birth of a grandson. Setting out for England he found however, he had acquired not only a horse, but a man and a cat besides!"

Calista then related how unfortunately, when they arrived in England and the stallion recovered his former beauty, his rich bay coat gleaming with health, he refused to be handled or mounted by anyone but Agba.

This refusal took the form of displaying active and vicious resentment, and after several would-be riders had been injured, Mr. Coke's patience ran out!

At this point in the story Calista clasped her hands together.

"Once again," she said with a sob in her voice, "the magnificent animal and loyal Agba fell on bad times.

"Their new owner, a Mr. Rodgers, was beating the horse when Agba attacked him for doing so. Agba was arrested and thrown into Newgate Prison.

"Then once again fate changed everything!"

Calista told the Earl that the story of the horse and the little dark-skinned man who loved him so passionately was related to Sarah Jennings, the Duchess of Marlborough, and because it touched her heart she brought her son-in-law Lord Godolphin, to Newgate and they succeeded in getting Agba released.

The Bedouin took them to the stable which housed Scham and Lord Godolphin, interested in Arab stock, bought the stallion from Mr. Rodgers.

Lord Godolphin was, as it happened, not particularly impressed with his new purchase. He turned Scham loose in the fields and really forget about him.

But Agba believed in Scham's destiny which to him was declared by the sign of a white crescent on the coronet just above his off hind foot.

Secretly the Bedouin manœuvred Scham — now known as Godolphin Arabian because in those days horses took their master's name — into serving Roxana, a great mare!

When it was discovered Scham and Agba were banished to an outlying estate, until Roxana's foal called Lath, developed into such an outstanding horse that Agba was recalled.

Calista gave a deep sigh and said:

"You know the rest of the story," she went on. "Do you not think it the most thrilling, exciting history you have ever heard?"

Painful though it was, the Earl smiled.

"I am indeed glad to have heard it."

"Godolphin Arabian died at the age of

twenty-nine," Calista finished, "just after the death of the cat. Agba followed them soon afterwards."

It was a story that Calista was to return to and discuss in the days that followed.

As the Earl got better he found himself being amused in a way he had never known before by Calista's excitement and enthusiasm over the horses and the stories she would tell him about them.

The days passed leisurely until one morning Calista came in after she had been exercising the horses with a newspaper in her hand.

She rode twice every day, for an hour and a half in the morning on Centaur, and for the same length of time in the afternoon on Orestes.

The Earl, as soon as he could speak authoritatively, insisted on her promising him that she would not go beyond the fields which adjoined the Inn.

"If you are afraid the Circus folk will see me," Calista said, "they left the night we came here and they would never make trouble or ask too many questions about people's private lives."

"The man who attacked me might be

looking for you," the Earl said.

He saw a shadow pass over Calista's face and he asked:

"How could you have done anything so wild — so crazy — as to go away by yourself without any form of protection and I gather, without money?"

"That, I admit, was very stupid of me," Calista replied. "I forgot I should need money."

"It is a useful commodity in any circumstances," the Earl said dryly, "but especially when one is amongst strangers."

Calista smiled.

"That is why I was glad to see that your purse was well filled when we came here! But what would you have done if footpads had picked your pocket?"

"I expect I should have managed," the Earl replied.

Calista put her head a little on one side as she looked at him.

"I have a feeling you would always manage. That is not something I would say of most rich people!"

"I am glad you have such a high opinion of my capabilities," the Earl answered, "which is more than I have of yours! You had no right to disappear as you did!"

Calista did not meet his eyes.

"I felt it was the only thing I could do. I was so ashamed of Mama's behaviour!"

"Did you have any idea of her plans?" the Earl asked.

"I felt that as you were leaving the next day time was running out," Calista replied. "So she was certain to try a trick of some sort to get us into each other's arms."

"So you pretended to have a cold?"

"That is right. I waited until Mama had gone down to dinner before I let her know I had retired to bed. I thought there would be nothing she could do about us, if I stayed upstairs! But she outwitted me!"

"How did she manage it?" the Earl enquired.

"When the ladies left the gentlemen in the Dining-Room," Calista answered. "Mama came up to my bedroom with a glass of medicine in her hand!"

" 'I do not believe you have a cold, Calista,' she said. 'I am certain you could have made an effort to come downstairs for dinner tonight. I know you want to go

221

to the races tomorrow, so unless you drink this rather nasty, but very effective tisane, you you stay in bed and I will not permit you to leave the house!' "

Calista paused.

"I have tasted Mama's tisanes before, and they are indeed very unpleasant! But I would have drunk anything rather than miss the races!"

"So you drank what obviously was a sleeping-draught?"

"I drank it also because I thought there was nothing incriminating we could be tricked into doing on a racecourse," Calista answered. "Then as I finished the glass I saw a look in Mama's eyes which frightened me!"

" 'What have you given me?' I asked.

" 'Just something that will make you feel better!' she answered.

"She went from the room a few minutes later and I must have fallen asleep."

"I have to admit that your mother is very resourceful!" the Earl remarked.

"How could she do such a thing to me?" Calista asked. "I will never forgive her — never!"

"Someone must have carried you to my

room and put you in my bed," the Earl said, "and that could not have been your mother."

"I expect it was her lady's maids," Calista replied. "She has two of them — horrible creatures who always spied on us when we were children and told Mama everything we did. They would have obeyed her, even if she had asked them to cut me up into small pieces and throw me into the lake!"

She was silent for a moment, then she said anxiously:

"You did not think that I was in the plot?"

"Of course not!" the Earl answered. "But I still think, Calista, you should have stayed and faced the music rather than run away in that foolhardy manner."

"To tell you the truth, it was an adventure!" Calista smiled. "I wish you had seen how well Centaur acted when he was in the ring. The crowds used to go wild about him."

"I did see him," the Earl replied. "I watched your performance before I came to find you in your caravan."

"Centaur was good, was he not?"

"Magnificent!"

"Are you well enough now to hear rather bad news?" she asked anxiously.

"What can you have been up to now?" the Earl asked, but he did not sound very worried.

"Your horse, if you entered one, did not win the Gold Cup at Ascot!"

"Good Lord!" the Earl ejaculated. "I had forgotten Ascot! Who won it?"

"Lord George Bentinck's Grey Momus!"

"Good for George!" the Earl exclaimed. "No wonder he was keen that I should keep Delos for the St. Leger!"

"And the Duke of Portland's Bestian won the St. James's Palace Stakes. What happened to your horses?"

"To tell you the truth," the Earl replied, "I was so worried about you that I delayed entering either Zeus or Pericles as I had intended, so neither of them ran."

"So it was my fault," Calista exclaimed. "With so much to account for to you, I cannot think why you even speak to me!"

"I find you a most efficient nurse."

"I am glad about that," she said in a low voice "because I am very apologetic for upsetting your life — I am really!"

"I dare say my rivals were delighted not to see me at Ascot, and that my horses also stayed away!" the Earl answered lightly.

"But you would have won the Gold Cup," Calista said miserably. "And the Queen was there. It described her appearance in the newspapers."

"You can spare me the social gossip," the Earl said. "I would rather hear some more of your stories about the Arabians and the Barbs."

"I know a lot," Calista replied. "Some of the tales I have told you are, I suspect, fictitious, but I have been trying to collect every bit of information I could about horses ever since I was fifteen. One day I would like to show you a Scrapbook I have made, copying out information from books, old newspapers and the tales the grooms have told me."

She paused.

"But I shall never be able to show it to you, will I . . . if I do not go home?"

"Of course you are going home," the Earl said firmly. "I will take you back and I think your mother will be so pleased

225

to see you that she will not be angry."

"How can you be sure of that?"

"Your mother was genuinely worried about you, Calista, and she told me that of all her children she loved you the best because you most resembled your father."

Calista's eyes widened, then she said:

"If you had told me that three years ago I should have been so thrilled. I loved and admired Mama then, and I longed for her to love me, but now. . ."

"Now?" the Earl prompted as she did not continue.

"I can never forgive her for trying to force us into marriage; for drugging me and for trying to trap you in that under-hand and horrible manner!"

She paused before she asked:

"Were you disgusted? Or were you furiously angry?"

The Earl smiled.

"I think at the time I was so bewildered and surprised that I was not consciously as angry as I ought to have been. It was the sheer audacity of the whole plan which took my breath away."

"What must Lord George and Lord Palmerston have thought?"

"They did not tell me."

"But you must have a good idea."

"If I have, I am not going to relate it to you," the Earl answered. "I will take you home, Calista, as soon as I am well enough to travel, and I am quite certain that very few people will know of this escapade."

He saw the expression on her face and said:

"Good God, girl! You cannot ruin your whole life simply because your mother staged a remarkable theatrical performance and won a thousand guineas for doing so."

Calista stared at him for a moment, then she rose to her feet to walk across the room to the window.

"Are you seriously suggesting," she asked in a strangled voice, "that I should marry you?"

"Quite frankly, we have no alternative," the Earl replied. "And as we get along extremely well together, Calista, I have a feeling that our marriage will be a very pleasant one."

She did not answer and after a moment he went on:

"We have so many things in common, especially horses. I think you will find a great deal to interest you in my plans for breeding from the stallions I have already put out to grass and also in my racing-stables."

He smiled before he continued:

"With your encouragement I might even breed a horse which would win 862 races like Eclipse, or 1042 like King Herod."

"That would be an achievement!" Calista agreed in a low voice. "But at the same time you could do it all quite well without me."

"I think it would be amusing for us both to do things together," the Earl said. "And quite frankly, Calista, I can say in all truth that if I have to marry someone I would rather it were you than anyone else I have ever met."

"Thank you," Calista answered. "But you know as well as I do that it is not the same as being in love."

"How do you know if you have never been in love?"

"We both know in our minds, or perhaps in our hearts what it should be like."

"Nevertheless," the Earl said, "I am convinced that a marriage based on mutual trust, on shared interests, and most of all on an intelligent determination to make each other happy should be successful."

Calista did not answer and he lay back against his pillows watching the afternoon sun picking out the red lights in her hair.

He felt that she was unhappy and ill-at-ease, but for the moment he decided to say no more and not even try to persuade her that she must do what was right.

He had a feeling that she was like a horse that was not yet broken in to the bridle and therefore must be coaxed, rather than compelled, to do what was required.

There was, he thought, quite apart from her courage and her defiance of convention, which were very much a part of her character, a sensitivity and an idealism about her that he had never noticed before in any other woman he had known.

'She feels things much more deeply than she will ever admit,' the Earl thought to himself, and found himself wondering exactly what she felt about him.

For the first time in his life he was not quite sure about his relationship with a woman.

6

"It is your move!" the Earl said.

Calista started as if her thoughts had been far away, then concentrated on the chessboard and realized that she was in a vulnerable position.

"What were you thinking about?" the Earl asked after a moment.

She smiled at him.

"I was thinking about Orestes, and wondering whether you intended to breed from him."

"Do you think about nothing except horses?" the Earl asked and there was a touch of irritation in his voice.

"They fascinate me," Calista replied. "I was thinking last night how stupid I was not to have asked Coco to give me the French book in which I found the story of Godolphin Arabian. There were other tales in it which I should have liked to read to you."

She paused as if trying to recall them,

then she said:

"Coco would have given it to me because. . ."

She stopped and after a moment the Earl prompted:

"Because of what?"

"Oh, nothing," she said lightly looking down at the chessboard.

"I think you were about to say because he was in love with you," the Earl remarked after a moment. "That is the truth, is it not?"

He watched Calista's face and saw the colour come into her cheeks.

"Yes, it is true," she replied after a moment, "but he was very kind and did not frighten me as Manzani did."

"Did he kiss you?"

The Earl's voice was sharp.

"Of course not!"

"Then how do you know he was in love with you? Did he tell you so?"

"I . . . it was . . . obvious in the way he did things for me, and the manner in which he . . . spoke. I knew he realized that our backgrounds were very different and I was not an . . . ordinary Circus performer."

"He would have been half-witted if he had thought otherwise," the Earl said. "But I want to know about this love-affair."

"It was not a love-affair," Calista replied hotly, "and you have no right to question me."

"I have every right and as your future husband I am naturally interested."

Calista was silent. Then she said:

"One always thinks of Clowns as being coarse, vulgar people. A lot of them were, but Coco was . . . different, perhaps because he was . . . French."

"How was he different?" the Earl asked insistently.

"I . . . I cannot quite . . . explain," Calista replied, "not . . without sounding conceited."

"Try!"

"Well. ." she said as if she was feeling for words, "I believe Coco thought I was his . . . ideal. He read a lot and he loved poetry. He recited some to me and the poems were always about a man striving for the unobtainable . . . for something that he recognized with his heart and soul . . . but felt he would never . . find."

"So you think you were to this man Coco what he had been seeking?"

Calista did not answer.

She looked away towards the sunshine coming in through the window.

"I asked you a question," the Earl said after a moment.

"I did not know it was so . . . painful to hurt anyone," Calista murmured. "When I said good-bye to Coco after he brought you here, the pain in his eyes was almost . . .unbearable."

"He brought me here?" the Earl asked.

"How else did you think I managed to get you away from the Circus? I knew that Manzani, when he regained consciousness, would want to kill you!"

"Why was he unconscious?"

"Because I hit him on the back of the head with a tent-peg."

The Earl stared at her incredulously.

"When he knocked you out," she explained, "he would have gone on hitting and kicking you. Manzani was like that when he lost his temper."

"So you rendered him unconscious!"

"I . . . I had an iron tent-peg just . . . inside the caravan."

"Why?"

Her eyes flickered and after a moment she said:

"I was afraid."

"Of him?"

"Yes . . . he had tried the door of my caravan the previous night. I had bolted it but it was not very strong, and he could . . easily have . . broken in."

The Earl was silent, then he said:

"So the Clown saved you as I was unable to do."

"I saved myself!" Calista retorted. "But the difficulty was to get you away. Coco fetched your horse and, with the help of the small boy who was holding Orestes for you, we lifted you onto him. Then Coco rode behind you and supported you in the saddle until we reached the Inn."

"I suppose I should be grateful to him," the Earl said somewhat reluctantly.

"He did not want your gratitude," Calista answered. "He did it for me."

"That is obvious!"

The Earl's eyes were on Calista's face as he went on:

"I imagine this is the first time that you have had a man in love with you, or at least been aware he was. What did you feel?"

Calista considered the question almost as if it was an impersonal one.

"I think I felt . . . honoured and rather flattered," she said after a moment. "At the same time I felt desperately sorry that I must hurt him."

"Were you certain from the very first that was what you would have to do?" the Earl enquired. "Or did you think perhaps at the beginning that you might reciprocate his love?"

"I did not think so, but not because as you might imagine he was a Clown," Calista answered. "Coco was the son of a French lawyer. His father wished him to go into his Chambers, or whatever they call them in France, and he had agreed to do so."

She gave a little sigh.

"Coco's father was however a brutal man who knocked his mother about. He did this once too often and Coco attacked him, wounding and almost killing him!"

"He sounds as dangerous a character as your other admirer!" the Earl said sarcastically.

"Coco was only defending his mother," Calista said quickly. "He was actually quiet, gentle and poetical. When he realized that his father was badly injured, he knew he could no longer stay at home. So he left, intending to go on the stage."

Again Calista sighed.

"He told me how he trudged from theatre to theatre without success, and then he thought of joining a Circus. After working in one in France for a year he heard that one of the turns was coming to England to appear in The Great Carno's Circus, and he joined them. He was a good actor. The Boss appreciated him."

"As you did," the Earl said.

Calista made a gesture with her hands.

"He was an educated man as few of the others were—most of them were unable to read or write — and I suppose it was inevitable that we should find something in common with each other."

"Allied to the fact that you are a very lovely young woman," the Earl said and again his voice was sarcastic.

"I have a feeling that you are criticizing me," Calista said after a moment. "It was not my fault that Coco fell in love with me

237

or that Manzani forced his attentions on me."

"Not your fault? Whose fault was it that you were in the Circus at all? Can you imagine what sort of trouble you might have been in if you had stayed any longer?"

Calista did not answer and the Earl asked:

"Do you imagine that the poetical Coco would have been able to save you from Manzani?"

He saw by the expression on her face that she had thought of this for herself.

"I never envisaged . . complications of that . . sort," she faltered. "When The Boss suggested that Centaur and I should join his Circus it seemed a Heaven-sent opportunity to earn money and to hide from Mama."

She looked at the Earl and added accusingly:

"Mama would never have found me. I cannot think why you had to interfere!"

"Are you still so naive as not to realize it was a godsend I came when I did?" the Earl enquired. "Did you understand what Manzani was asking of you?"

"He was asking me to . . live with him as if I . . were his . . wife," Calista replied hesitatingly, "and that is . . something I would . . never have done . . because I hated him!"

"Would you have had any choice?"

Her eyes flickered and her face was very pale as she said:

"I always imagined, when I lived at home, that I could . . look after . . myself, but it was . . frightening being on my own."

"That is something you will never be again," the Earl said, "and I think, Calista, when you say your prayers, which I fancy you do, you should say one of gratitude that you have come out of this regrettable episode unscathed!"

"All the same I do not regret it!" Calista answered. "I learned a lot about people; about their kindness, their courage and their endurance! I saw too how genuinely the majority of the performers cared for their animals."

Her voice was warm as she continued:

"For instance, the man who tamed the tigers really loved them, and although they snarled and looked ferocious in the ring, they would let him sit with them in their cages, and he would brush their coats and talk to them while he did so."

She smiled.

"The Circus people call such wild animals 'cats' and that is exactly how they behave!"

"While I find you extremely irresponsible," the Earl said, "I have to admire your courage. I can imagine no other woman of my acquaintance who would work in a Circus and actually find it agreeable."

"I loved hearing Centaur being applauded," Calista confessed, "and there was something very thrilling when the children screamed with delight as he carried away the bag of gold and gave it to the poor, ragged man."

"How did you teach him to do that?"

"Centaur understands everything I say to him."

The Earl laughed.

"I am quite certain of one thing Calista, that any man who falls in love with you, including your husband, will find his most serious rival is Centaur!"

Calista looked at him a little uncertainly

and as if to make amends for his inter-
rogation he said:

"You say the Circus people call the
wild animals 'cats'. I believe they have a
language of their own."

"Coco explained it to me," Calista
replied. "In every country the Circus has
its own language, which is jealously
guarded."

"Why?" the Earl enquired.

"So that they can discuss their private
affairs in front of *'flatties'* which means
outsiders, like you, and you would not
know what they were saying."

"I can quite see this is another entry for
your Scrapbook," the Earl smiled. "Tell
me some of the words."

"Performing dogs are known as *slang-
ing-buffers'*," Calista answered. " *'Palari'*
means to talk, while a woman is known as
a *'Dona'*."

"I can guess the origin of some of those
words," the Earl said.

"Coco said that the Circus language in
England is a mixture of Romany, Italian,
rhyming slang and back-slang, and the
Romany language, of course, is of Orien-
tal origin."

"I knew that," the Earl said. "Tell me some more words."

" *'Denari'* means money," Calista answered. " *'Cushy'* for easy is directly derived from the Romany for 'good' and when there were Gypsies in the Circus they said *'grei'* instead of 'horse', but most of the Circus folk call them *'prads'*."

She gave a little laugh.

"I suppose really I am breaking their code of honour in telling you this and I am sure Coco would not approve. All Clowns, by the way, are called *'Joeys'*."

"Did you tell Coco who you were?" the Earl enquired.

"No."

"Why not? Unless you did not trust him?"

"It was not that. It was because I thought it might sound rather like boasting to say I had run away from home because my mother wished me to marry an Earl! When he found you unconscious and asked me who you were, I said you were my husband!"

"That was sensible," the Earl approved, "and it was only anticipating what will become a fact."

Calista rose from the bed on which she had been sitting to play chess with the Earl and walked towards the window.

He watched her in silence and after a moment she said:

"The Doctor said you could get up to-morrow and you would be well enough to travel in a carriage."

"I know that," the Earl said, "but I want to feel I am strong again and truly on my feet before we go back to confront your mother and face the congratulations."

"Must we do that?" Calista asked in a low voice.

"Unless you wish to stay for ever in the obscurity of this Inn, or others like it?"

"You want to get back to your Estates, your horses, and of course your political life."

The Earl did not reply and after a moment she said:

"Have you forgotten the Coronation will take place on the 28th — a week from now?"

"I had forgotten it," the Earl answered. "I cannot say it is an event to which I am looking forward."

"You will certainly need to be well for it."

"I agree. Five hours in the Abbey will be a feat of endurance for anyone!"

"You will be well enough by then," Calista said confidently.

"I hope so," he replied.

"I have been thinking," she said slowly, "that we need not tell anyone that you have been injured or forced to stay in bed. You can pretend that all the time you have been away you have been looking for me and actually found me only on the day that we returned home."

"I see you are determined to save my face."

"I . . I was not only thinking of you. I know how angry Mama would be if she thought I had been living here in this Inn without a Chaperon."

"I am quite sure your mother would be only too delighted to have another and very plausible reason to insist upon our marrying each other with all possible speed!" the Earl said scathingly.

He spoke without thinking, but when he saw the expression in Calista's eyes and the colour flooding into her cheeks he wished he had been more tactful.

"Mama would think. ." Calista began. "Oh . . no! How could she?"

"We must be careful to give her no reason for thinking anything of the sort," the Earl said soothingly.

He saw that Calista still looked shocked and after a moment he said:

"You are very young, but you must realize by now that the world is full of pitfalls for an innocent girl, and that it is easy for people's motives and actions to be misinterpreted."

"Yes . . . I know," Calista replied, "and I suppose that as there have been so many lovely and attractive women in your life . . people would assume that because we have been alone . . together you would naturally . . make love to me."

"I am sure that is something you too would have expected," the Earl said with a smile, "if I had not been a helpless invalid, relying on you not as a woman, but as a nurse."

He spoke teasingly. Then in a very low voice Calista said:

"May I ask you . . something?"

"But of course," he replied. "I think by

now we both realize, Calista, that there is nothing we cannot discuss together without embarrassment."

"You will not be . . angry, or think I am . . prying into your . . private affairs?"

"You may ask me anything you wish," the Earl replied, "and I will answer you as honestly as I can."

"Then are you . . very much in . . love with Lady Genevieve Rodney?"

The Earl knew he should have anticipated the question, and yet he had put Lady Genevieve so completely out of his mind after her blatant attempt to cheat him that it came as quite a shock to hear Calista's question.

At the same time he realized it was obvious she would have known about Genevieve.

The smart, society personalities that Lady Chevington entertained would have chattered and gossiped about them and it would be impossible to deny the association especially as Genevieve had taken good care that their names were commonly linked together.

Pushing himself up a little higher against his pillows the Earl said:

"Come back here, Calista! I want to talk to you."

He thought for a moment she would disobey him, but she turned from the window and walked slowly and, he thought, somewhat reluctantly towards his bed.

"Sit down!" he ordered.

She obeyed him sitting where she had been sitting before on the side of the mattress facing him, the chessboard between them.

"I want to try to explain something to you," the Earl began, "and I think it important from the point of view of our future happiness and our relationship with each other."

Calista raised her grey-green eyes to his and he thought she looked not only very lovely but also so fragile and insubstantial that it was difficult to think of her as a grown woman of flesh and blood.

"I am much older than you," the Earl went on, "and I have lived what people call a 'full life'. I would not insult your intelligence, Calista, by pretending that I have not had many love-affairs."

He paused, before he said:

"But I want you to believe me when I say that they have never on my part been anything more serious than interludes of great enjoyment and pleasure."

"Are you trying to tell me that you never wished any of the ladies you . . loved to . . become your . . wife?" Calista asked in a low voice.

"That is exactly what I am trying to say," the Earl replied. "I never envisaged any of them taking the place of my mother at Helstone House, or bearing my name."

"But did they not want to marry you?"

The Earl knew that Calista was thinking of Lady Genevieve.

"Women always want to tie a man down; to capture him; to make him their own possession. But I have always wanted to be free."

"You are not . . now," Calista said in an unhappy little voice.

"That is different, as we both know," the Earl answered, "but what we are discussing at the moment, Calista, is whether while marrying you my heart is engaged elsewhere. I can answer that question in all truthfulness: it is not!"

"Thank you for . . telling me."

As if Calista decided that the conversation was now at an end, she picked up the chessboard and took it from the bed to a table on the other side of the room.

"I will go and see if the newspapers have arrived," she said. "There is one that comes from London on the afternoon Stage-coach and there might be something of interest in it."

"Why not ring the bell?" the Earl suggested.

"I would rather go myself."

"I believe that is merely an excuse to see how Centaur is faring."

Calista laughed.

"You are too perceptive. I do in fact want to see if he has been properly fed and has enough hay."

"I have already warned you, I shall be jealous of that animal!" the Earl said.

Calista laughed again.

"Centaur is far more likely to be jealous of you," she answered and going from the room shut the door behind her.

The Earl stared after her before settling himself comfortably down against the pillows.

She was an extraordinary girl, he

decided. Even after having been alone with her for so long, he found it difficult to guess what she was thinking.

He had had no idea that anyone so young could have such an interest in subjects which did not usually appeal to women, especially beautiful ones. It amazed him.

At the same time he was appalled when he thought of the risks Calista had run being alone in the Circus.

He found himself wondering what would have happened if he had not arrived at exactly the right moment.

He supposed that she would have cried out for help and perhaps The Boss, as she had told him the owner was called, would have made Manzani behave himself.

At the same time it had been a risk which no girl brought up as Calista had been should encounter.

The Earl also found himself wondering about Coco.

Had the Frenchman really loved her without demands for anything more intimate than a kiss on her hand?

He could hardly believe it possible, but then the Earl remembered that the women who had been attracted to him and whom he found desirable had always made it quite clear from the very beginning of their acquaintance exactly what they expected of him.

He could hardly believe it possible that he would have a relationship with a young and beautiful girl which would seem to be entirely platonic.

He realized of course that he was an invalid and there could be no question of any advances coming from him.

But Calista treated him in a friendly, almost comradely fashion, and did not in any way intrude her femininity upon their relationship.

The women whom the Earl had known in the past had flirted, often outrageously, not only in words, but also with the movements of their bodies.

Their eyes spoke an invitation and their lips would be provocative.

Calista simply talked to him as though he were another woman, or perhaps her horse.

"She is completely unawakened," he told himself, and wondered if the red in her hair denoted a fire within her which one day would be aroused to a flaming desire.

He asked himself too how those grey-green eyes would look if they held in them an expression of love, and then he found himself wondering if her lips, which had never been kissed, would be soft and yielding.

He decided the prospect of being married to Calista no longer annoyed him.

The anger he had felt when he realized that his hand had been forced by Lady Chevington placing Calista in his bed had evaporated.

Now he found himself planning with his usual efficiency that they would be married before the end of the summer.

It would be a very grand wedding, either at St. James's, Piccadilly, or at St. George's, Hanover Square.

The Queen, he hoped would be one of the guests and the Church would be packed not only with all his social acquaintances, but also his Parliamentary ones.

The tenants would come up from Helstone House in the country and he would arrange for them to have on their return home, a wedding celebration in the shape of a feast.

An ox would be roasted whole, there would be great barrels of ale, and of course fireworks to complete the evening's entertainment.

To the Earl's surprise he found himself positively looking forward to his marriage and all it entailed, without resentment and indeed without much rancour towards his future mother-in-law.

He determined however that Lady Chevington would not be a frequent guest, either at his house in London, or in the country.

He felt she was a bad influence where Calista was concerned.

It was not only her determination to marry her daughters off to important husbands, but also the way she had allowed Calista to be too much on her own; to run wild and for instance to walk about in pantaloons, wearing a jockey's jacket.

'She will have to be more circumspect as my wife,' the Earl decided.

·   ·   ·

Calista dined alone, as she had done every evening, in the parlour downstairs.

When she came back to the Earl's bedroom the valet had taken the tray away, but he still had a bottle of Champagne beside his bed in a wine-cooler and he was sipping it from a glass which he held in his hand.

"I am drinking a toast to tomorrow!" he told Calista as she came in through the door.

She had changed from the muslin dress she had worn all day into her other one. She had only the two which she wore alternately.

They were very simple, and yet with their full skirts and her very tiny waist they became her.

She moved with what the Earl privately thought was the grace of a swan across the room towards him.

"What is your toast?"

"Tomorrow!" he replied. "When I take up my life again!"

"I think I am frightened of tomorrow," Calista said. "Staying here has been like living on a small island in a little world of our own with nobody to encroach upon us."

"Has that made you happy?"

"Yes, I have been happy. It has been wonderful to feel free; to have nobody scolding or finding fault, and . . ."

She gave him a smile which illuminated her face.

". . . to have two such superb horses to ride!"

"So we have come back to the horses!" the Earl said dryly. "But you have forgotten something very important."

"What is that?" Calista asked.

"Me!" he replied. "What I really wanted to know, Calista, is if you have been happy with me?"

"I have," she answered. "Very happy! I enjoy talking to you. I like hearing all the things you can tell me and I like being with you."

She spoke unaffectedly, almost unthinkingly. Then as her eyes met his she was suddenly very still.

She was looking at him and he was looking at her and it seemed as if something magnetic passed between them.

"Calista!" the Earl exclaimed and his voice was deep.

They were interrupted by a knock on

the door and without waiting for an answer the valet who looked after the Earl came into the room.

"Th' Master wants ter know, Sir, as ye be a-coming down for luncheon tomorrow, whether ye'd fancy a nice piece of pork or whether ye be more partial to a saddle o' mutton?"

"That, of course, is a very important decision," the Earl said. "I think, on the whole, the saddle of mutton!"

"Thank ye, Sir. I'll tell the Master."

The valet went from the room and Calista laughed.

"They are obviously getting ready to celebrate your arrival downstairs, prompted largely by Mrs. Blossom, the Inn-keeper's wife. She told me today that you were a 'proper gentleman' and so handsome that she would be 'real worret' if she were married to you herself!"

"Was she warning you?" the Earl asked.

"I have a feeling she was," Calista replied. "But then she added, I am sure for the sake of my morale, that both her husband and son thought I was prettier than the Queen herself!"

"I should hope so!" the Earl exclaimed. "You do not admire Queen Victoria?"

"Not particularly. She will grow fat and heavy as she gets older. That type always does."

"I have a feeling that by being so critical you are committing *lèse majesté*," Calista laughed, "and, as you have a long day before you tomorrow, I suggest you retire early as I intend to do."

The Earl put down the glass onto the table beside the bed and held out his hand.

"Good-night, Calista!" he said. "I want to thank you for looking after me so well. I know of no-one else who would have achieved it more charmingly and at the same time look very much prettier than the Queen!"

Calista put her hand in his and his fingers closed over hers as he continued:

"You have in fact been wonderfully kind and I am very grateful. I only hope I have not lost all your respect by playing such an unglamorous part in my attempt to save you."

"We said we would not speak about it to anyone else," Calista said, "and I think we should forget about it too."

"Are you saving my pride?" the Earl asked with a hint of laughter in his voice.

"I think you were very brave!" Calista answered. "But the odds were against you."

"Nevertheless it was an ignominious defeat," the Earl said still holding her hand. "But perhaps to be a failure sometimes is good for the soul — at least I am sure Lord Yaxley would think so."

"Why him particularly?"

"He thinks I am too successful and too pleased with myself," the Earl answered. "At the moment I am neither!"

"One cannot win every race."

"That is true," he asnwered, "but together we will try for the Classics. Is that a deal?"

He did not wait for an answer but raised her hand to his lips.

She felt his mouth warm against her skin, then he said quietly:

"I shall be able to thank you more effectively tomorrow, when I am on my feet."

Calista drew her hand away from his.

"Good-night," she said shyly.

"Good-night, Calista."

She moved to the fireplace to pull at the bell which would summon the valet, and with another little smile she went towards the communicating door which lay between their two rooms.

"I have been very happy!" she said in a low voice.

Then before the Earl could respond the door closed behind her.

.   .   .

The Earl was aroused by the curtains being drawn back smoothly and quietly from the window.

He had been asleep, but the sound brought him back to consciousness and he was aware of the sunlight flooding in through the diamond-paned casement to cast a golden glow over the whole room.

Through the open window came the song of the birds, and the sweet fragrance of the roses growing up the side of the Inn, and of the stocks planted in the garden below.

"Good-morning, M'Lord," a familiar voice said.

259

The Earl started and stared in astonishment to see not the hotel servant he had expected but his own valet.

"Good God, Travis!" he ejaculated. "What are you doing here?"

"Mr. Grotham received Your Lordship's note late last night, and very glad we were to hear from you, M'Lord. It's worried we've been, and that's a fact!"

"Mr. Grotham received my note?" the Earl repeated slowly.

"Yes, M'Lord, and I brought the travelling carriage which Your Lordship ordered and the extra groom to ride back Orestes."

The Earl said nothing and after a moment Travis went on:

" 'Tis hard to believe that Your Lordship should have had a riding accident, seeing that Your Lordship's horsemanship is equalled by none! But as the grooms were saying — that stallion's a tricky customer!"

Travis tidied a few objects in the room before he said:

"I brought Your Lordship some fresh clothes with me. I can imagine the condition of the ones you've been wearing for so long."

"Knock at that door!" the Earl commanded pointing his finger.

He spoke so sharply that Travis looked surprised. Nevertheless he walked quickly to the communicating door and knocked.

There was no reply.

"Open it!" the Earl said. "Tell me what is inside."

Travis did as he was told.

"It is empty, M'Lord. The bed's been slept in, but there's no-one in here now."

"Is there anything hanging in the wardrobe?" the Earl asked.

Travis entered the room and the Earl heard a cupboard being opened. It was followed by the sound of drawers being pulled out and shut again.

The valet came back to the bedroom.

"No, M'Lord."

The Earl pushed back the bedclothes.

"I want to get up," he said. "Fetch my clothes and when I am dressed I want to see the Landlord."

A quarter of an hour later he was speaking alone with the Landlord.

"Where is my wife?"

The Landlord looked surprised.

"I thought, Sir, you'd be aware that Mrs. Helstone left the Inn early this morning. She tells me she were going ahead to have everything in readiness for your return to London. Is anything wrong?"

"No," the Earl said quickly. "I was just not expecting her to leave while I was still asleep."

"Mrs. Helstone left before six o'clock, Sir. I feel sure she didn't wish to disturb you."

The Landlord glanced over his shoulder before he added:

"I didn't like to mention it, Sir, but she said that when the carriage arrived she didn't wish me to tell 'em that she'd gone ahead. She wished it to be a surprise."

"Yes, that was quite right," the Earl agreed hastily. "My wife would not want our London servants to think she was interfering or finding fault. You will oblige me, Landlord, if you will not speak of the fact that she has left, or indeed that she has been here."

The Earl thought that the Landlord looked at him suspiciously but as he asked for the bill and added an over

262

generous gratuity the Landlord was prepared to agree to anything.

The Earl found it no effort to go downstairs and the journey to London in his well-sprung carriage was not over-fatiguing.

At the same time he was desperately worried about Calista.

He tried to convince himself that she had in fact just done as she had told the Landlord and gone ahead so that her mother would not learn that they had been together in the Inn. In which case he would find her waiting for him in London.

It was a plausible explanation, but it did not account for the fact that she had not taken him into her confidence and he had the uneasy feeling, which proved to be justified, that when he arrived she would not be there.

He did not visit Lady Chevington personally but sent a message from Helstone House to enquire if she had news of Calista.

Lady Chevington appeared less than an hour later.

"You have been away so long, My Lord," she said, "I thought you must have found Calista by now."

"You have not heard from her your-self?" the Earl replied evasively.

"If I had I would have done my best to get in touch with you," Lady Chevington answered. "Where can she be? Surely if she has been involved in an accident or was dead we would have learned of it somehow?"

"One imagines it would be very difficult to disappear, especially riding such a distinctive horse," the Earl said.

"That is what I have been telling my-self," Lady Chevington sighed. "And it has been more difficult than I can ever tell you not to confide in my friends; not to ask for their help in finding Calista."

"You have not admitted to anyone that she has disappeared?" the Earl ques-tioned.

"Of course not!" Lady Chevington replied. "Can you imagine what the gossip would be like, and the speculation as to what she could be doing alone?"

She made an exasperated sound.

"No-one would credit that she was alone!"

"I thought that myself," the Earl

admitted.

"Then what can we do?"

"I intend now to do what we should have done in the first place," he said in a hard voice. "I know of an ex-Bow Street Runner who can put me in touch with a number of men who would undertake the search privately without involving the police. I shall employ a dozen of them and see how quickly they can discover Calista's whereabouts."

He did not tell Lady Chevington that he was almost certain Calista was somewhere in London.

He had ascertained before he left the Inn that she had taken the London road which ran through Barnet and Finchley.

Surely, he told himself, it would be difficult for her to pass through so many villages without being noticed?

Robinson arrived almost as soon as Lady Chevington had left.

The Earl gave him his instructions and told him in confidence that he had been right in his first suggestion that Calista might have joined a Circus.

"You don't think she'd join another one, M'Lord?" Robinson asked.

"I have a feeling that if she wishes to disappear again she will not do the obvious," the Earl replied. "She would know that I would look for her in Circuses as I looked before, so I am sure she will find some other place for herself and her horse."

"It'll not be easy, unless she has money, M'Lord," Robinson said.

The Earl knew, although he saw no reason to say so, that Calista had in fact more money now than when she had set out originally from her home at Epsom.

When he had paid the landlord's bill he had found tucked amongst the notes in his purse a small piece of paper. On it was written:

"I.O.U. £10. Calista."

At first he could hardly credit that after the days they had spent together and after he had told her so firmly and forcefully that she had behaved in a crazy, irresponsible fashion in going off on her own, Calista would in fact deny him and disappear once again.

He found it so hard to believe that, despite the I.O.U., he sent a groom without mentioning it to Lady Chevington, to Epsom to see if by any chance Calista had turned up at her home.

That night when he went to bed he found it impossible to sleep.

It was incredible that he was back where he had started, looking for a needle in a haystack, or one young girl and a horse.

He told himself that it was in fact a miracle that he had found her the first time and without her having suffered unduly from the experience.

How could he be sure that she would be so lucky again?

And why, he asked himself, should she have such a distaste of being married to him that she was prepared to suffer hardship and danger rather than submit to nothing more terrible than to be his wife?

It was a sobering thought that even now she would not accept the inevitable where he was concerned.

Surely there must be some other reason, he told himself, for her decision to ride away into the blue, having sent a groom from the Inn to his London house the night before.

He could hardly credit that they had talked as they had, that she had said good-night and told him she had been happy, knowing all the while that she intended to ride away at dawn.

He felt extremely angry that she should be so foolish and put him to so much trouble.

"Damn the girl!" he said out loud. "If this is what she wants of life, then I will forget about her!"

But suddenly, almost as if a voice told him so, he knew that was impossible.

7

The Earl walked into the Library and threw himself down into a chair. His riding-boots were dusty and he looked hot and tired.

He had been riding since early in the morning and had travelled many miles around the outskirts of London.

He had seen a hundred or more black horses with or without white stars on their noses, but nowhere had he caught a glimpse of a woman who looked anything like Calista.

"Would you care for any refreshment, M'Lord?" the Butler asked at his elbow.

"Bring me some brandy!"

When it came the Earl sipped the spirit slowly, staring across the room with unseeing eyes. Another day had passed and neither he nor the men he had employed through the ex-Bow Street Runner had found any clue to where Calista might be.

How could she vanish so completely?

he asked himself, and realized it was the question that had been repeating and repeating in his mind not only all day but also at night.

He had been unable to sleep and at last he had admitted to himself that his feelings for Calista were different from those he had known for any woman.

And yet it had been some days before he faced the fact that what he felt towards her was not anger, not indignation, not frustration, but love!

He thought again now as he had thought during the night that love had come to him at last in such a different guise from what he had expected.

Always before in his love-affairs he had been bemused by the desire of the senses, by his eagerness to possess a woman so that he had in fact had little time to consider anything but her physical attractions.

With Calista it was different.

He had fallen in love with her, he now believed, although he had no idea of it at the time, when they had talked beside the lake and she had said:

"Can you imagine what it would be like

to be here with someone you loved?"

Her voice had been soft and musical. Then she had finished her sentence with the words:

"And know that the stars were just wishes you had made for each other's happiness?"

"I must have known then," the Earl told himself, "that was what I wanted a woman to feel about me."

A woman who would care for his happiness rather than for her own! And yet he had been fool enough to talk to Calista as if their marriage was to be a business contract.

How could he have spoken so pompously about "having many things in common", and "finding an interest together in their horses" or that their marriage would be "based on mutual trust"?

"I must have been mad," the Earl said aloud.

He was sure now that what Calista wanted was that a man should say that he needed her as he had never needed another woman, that she meant everything in the world to him, and that he could not live without her.

He had never made such protestations in the past because they would not have been true; but now he was prepared to say them to a young girl called Calista who had run away from him because she had no desire to be his wife.

The door opened and the Butler said:

"Harwell would like to see you, M'Lord, if you can spare him a moment."

"What does he want?" the Earl asked impatiently.

Deep in his thoughts he resented the intrusion.

"Harwell, I understand, M'Lord, wishes to speak to you about a strange horse that has been left at the stables."

The Earl sat upright.

"A strange horse?" he repeated.

"Yes, M'Lord."

"Send Harwell in immediately!"

The Earl rose to his feet and waited until his Head-groom, a middle-aged man with a vast experience of horseflesh was brought to the Library.

The Butler shut the door behind him.

"What is it, Harewell?" the Earl enquired.

"I thought Your Lordship ought to know that about an hour ago a horse was brought to the stables."

"By whom?"

"A ragged boy led him in, M'Lord — the same boy as is always hanging about the Square trying to earn a copper or two."

"Did you ask him how he came by the horse?"

"I did, M'Lord. He informed me that a young lady gave him 2d to lead the animal into the Mews. I asked him if he knew who she was and he said he'd carried a note here for her once before."

The Earl remembered the note that Calista had sent him asking him to meet her by the Serpentine.

"Was there anything else?" he enquired.

"No, M'Lord. The horse is in good condition — but hungry."

The Earl was very still.

When he had given instructions about Centaur and Harwell had left, he walked across to the window to stare out onto the trees and shrubs in the centre of Berkeley Square.

"Why could I not have seen Calista?"
he asked himself.

Why had fate not been kind enough to
allow him a glimpse of her, when he had
ridden back from his long and fruitless
day of searching? He knew without being
told that she had parted with Centaur
only because she was desperate.

The horse was hungry!

He could not bear the thought that
Calista would be very much more hungry
than the animal she loved.

She must have spent the money she had
borrowed from him or perhaps it had
been stolen from her.

How could she defend herself against
the thieves, robbers and the pick-pockets
who abounded in London, especially at
the time of the Coronation?

"Hungry!" the Earl whispered to himself, and there was an expression of pain
and unhappiness in his eyes which had
never been there before.

.   .   .

The long service in the Abbey was
drawing to a close and the spectators of

the Coronation were nearly as exhausted as the Queen.

All London had been awakened at four in the morning by the sound of guns firing in the Park, and it had been impossible to get to sleep again on account of the noise of the people thronging the streets, the Bands and the marching troops.

The State Coach had carried the Queen at ten a.m. up Constitution Hill, along Piccadilly, down St. James's Street and across Trafalgar Square to Westminster Abbey.

The Peers and Peeresses had been told to be in their seats long before that, and travelling in their gilded and painted family coaches they had been cheered all along the route.

The Duke of Wellington had not only been acclaimed by the crowds, but was also cheered the whole way up the nave of the Abbey to the choir, and was moved to tears by his reception.

The Earl had gone to the Coronation reluctantly, but he had known that to be absent on such an auspicious occasion would cause a great deal of comment.

He thought too that his absence on top

of the fact that he had not been in London for two weeks, might give Lord Palmerston and Lord George Bentinck the idea that he was evading his honourable commitment to marry Calista.

Therefore, wearing his robes and carrying his coronet, he drove to Westminster Abbey with a scowl on his face which made several of his friends look at him apprehensively.

He had expected to be excessively bored, but like everyone else he could not help being impressed by the splendour of the crimson and gold Abbey.

The spectacle of the rows of Peeresses flashing with diamonds facing the Peers in their red and ermine robes, the magnificent copes of the Bishops, the altar laden with gold plate, were all breathtaking.

When the Queen appeared, a childish figure in the centre of the nave, the Earl forgot all he had ever said in criticism of her and felt there was something pathetic in her flower-like face. She had scarcely emerged from childhood, and yet she was taking upon herself the heavy responsibilities of a great Nation.

She seemed in his mind to be somehow linked with Calista, both of them young and immature, both of them having a poignant vulnerability which made a man long to protect them.

With a ray of sunshine falling on her head Victoria was crowned Queen of England. All the Peers and Peeresses put on their coronets, silver trumpets sounded and the Archbishop presented the Queen to the people, turning her to the east, west south and north.

The pageant reached its zenith with a tumult of waving flags and scarves, of huzzas and cheers.

As the Earl moved slowly with the other Peers towards the West Door he found Lord Palmerston at his side.

"I wonder if you would do me a favour, Helstone?" he enquired.

"Of course," the Earl answered.

"Would you be kind enough to accompany me at six o'clock to Hyde Park?"

The Earl looked surprised and Lord Palmerston explained:

"I have promised to be present at the ascent of Charles Green's balloon *The Royal Coronation*."

There was a pause while Lord Palmerston released his velvet robe which had become entangled with that of another Peer. Then he continued:

"I was present when Green made his first balloon ascent three years ago from Vauxhall Gardens. Count D'Orsay and I were very impressed with him then, and as you may know he is the first Aeronaut to use ordinary coal-gas."

"Yes, I remember hearing about it," the Earl remarked.

"Since then, Green crossed the Channel to come down in the Duchy of Nassau in Germany. Tonight he intends to carry a special report of Her Majesty's Coronation to Paris."

Lord Palmerston smiled before he said:

"If I were younger I think I would go with him! As it is, I am contenting myself with sending a formal message to my French *vis-à-vis* the Secretary of State for Foreign Affairs."

"Green has certainly made his mark amongst the Aeronauts," the Earl said, "although regrettably the French were ahead of us with their achievements in the skies."

"Green has been the most successful Englishman up to date," Lord Palmerston said, "and that is why I wish to encourage him. Will you help me speed him on his way? I do not like to ask a married man who would be with his family this evening."

"I shall be honoured to support you," the Earl said formally.

"Then I shall call for you at Helstone House at about a quarter to six," Lord Palmerston said.

They were parted by the crowd surging from the Abbey in search of their coaches.

Because Harwell was very experienced on State occasions the Earl found his coach easily and proceeded on his way home.

As he went he found it difficult not to worry about Calista, perhaps moving alone and unprotected amongst the huge crowds still lining the route, and to be afraid for her safety.

Incessantly into his mind came the knowledge that she must have been very desperate to part with Centaur.

He knew how deeply she loved her horse, and yet in a way it was some consolation for his aching heart to know that she had sent Centaur to him rather than to her mother.

Before he had left for the Abbey the Earl had visited his stables. As he patted Centaur's neck he wished that in addition to being half-human, as Calista believed, the horse could talk.

As Harwell had said, the animal was in good shape, but the Earl fancied that he was thinner than when he had last seen him at the Circus, and he wondered how quickly after she had left the Inn at Potters Bar Calista had lost the money she had taken with her.

"There appears to be nothing wrong with the horse," he said to his groom.

"No, M'Lord. It was just that last night he seemed unnaturally hungry."

"Feed him up."

"I will, M'Lord. Has Your Lordship any idea where he might have come from?"

"His name is Centaur," the Earl replied and walked back to the house.

Now as he returned from the Coronation and gave his long ermine-trimmed robe into the hands of the Butler, he hoped almost against hope that he would find a note from Calista waiting for him, but there was nothing.

As the Coronation ceremony had not ended until four-thirty and it had taken some time to get away from the Abbey, the Earl only just had time to change his clothes and be ready for Lord Palmerston when he arrived at a quarter to six.

Sitting back in the comfortable carriage of the Foreign Secretary the two men drove down Hill Street in silence until Lord Palmerston said what was uppermost in his mind.

"When do you intend to be married, Helstone?"

"Before the end of the summer."

"I rather expected to see Calista at the State Ball," Lord Palmerston remarked, "but as you were both absent I thought perhaps you were in the country."

"We were."

"Tell Calista that I shall be looking forward to her wedding, and I am hoping you will both like the present I have planned to give you."

"I am sure we shall appreciate it very greatly," the Earl said.

He was glad to see that they had only a short distance to go before reaching Hyde Park.

He did not wish to have to answer too many questions or make Lord Palmerston suspicious that he was inventing the answers.

For the Coronation, Hyde Park had been turned into a huge noisy, colourful fair-ground.

There was not only Richardson's Theatre, with all the best actors of the day performing Shakespearian dramas, there were menageries, Circuses, wax-works, and marionettes, besides a huge variety of peep-shows and roundabouts, freak and curiosity booths which exhibited every variety of ingenuity which could extract money from an astonished public.

As Lord Palmerston and the Earl drove towards the launching site of the balloon the latter looking around him saw signs advertising side-shows of fat men and women, spotted boys, fair Circassians, the Hottentot Venus, dwarfs, the two-headed lady, the Living Skeleton, learned pigs and fortune-telling ponies.

"If there is one exhibit which always

fascinates me," Lord Palmerston remarked, "it is the Pig-faced Lady!"

"I have always been told that she is in fact a brown bear, the paws and the face of which have been closely shaven," the Earl replied.

"That may be true," Lord Palmerston said. "I believe the white skin under the fur of bears has a close resemblance to that of a human being."

"We shall have to look for ourselves," the Earl smiled.

As he spoke they arrived at the open space in the centre of which was Charles Green's very impressive red and white striped balloon.

It was more elegant than most balloons in that the conventional wickerwork basket had been replaced by a boat-shaped car, painted red with gilded eagles' heads at the prow and stern. It was flying both the Union Jack and the flag of France.

Owing to the importance of the trip Green had inflated his balloon with more than the usual amount of coal-gas and besides the resisting power of the usual 56 lb weights, thirty-six policemen as well as twenty workmen had been hurriedly recruited to hold the balloon down.

The Royal Coronation which had previously been known as *The Royal Vauxhall* and *The Nassau*, was certainly extremely impressive as it strained at its moorings. Two thousand yards of the finest silk, imported from Italy in its raw state and made up in England, were swaying with every breath of wind.

When Lord Palmerston and the Earl arrived and walked to the platform which stood in front of the balloon they were greeted by the Lord Mayor of London with a number of other dignitaries, and introduced to Charles Green.

He was obviously delighted with the attention he was receiving, which the Earl felt he had fully earned.

He had not only made a great many ascents with passengers, but he had also recently been trying out scientific experiments and the previous year had actually reached a record altitude of 23,384 ft.

On his first cross-Channel journey he had risen to 13,000 ft. in five minutes.

"What will be your next target?" Lord Palmerston asked him.

"I hope to cross the Atlantic, My Lord," Charles Green replied.

"I hope you succeed," Lord Palmerston said. "It would be a great feather in England's cap if you were the first to do so."

When they had talked for a little while, after being introduced by the Lord Mayor to the assembled crowd, Lord Palmerston presented Charles Green with the letters he had prepared for the French Foreign Secretary and the Lord Mayor handed him descriptions and sketches of the Coronation for the Press in Paris.

As the speeches ended the Earl left the platform to examine the balloon.

The car seemed roomy and he noticed that to reduce the landing shock a grappling iron was fitted with an India rubber cord made in Paris.

He walked round the balloon to look at it from the other side and as he did so he realized that it was moored on the open grass near the Serpentine.

The sight of the silver water brought back to him all too vividly the day when in response to Calista's note he had met her, as she had requested, on the south side of the bridge and she had come galloping towards him on Centaur to throw herself at his feet.

Could anyone else have thought of anything so clever, he asked himself, as to pretend to fall from her horse so that she could speak to him without their meeting being made known to her mother?

She had been unpredictable ever since he had known her, and he felt a sudden longing that was a physical pain to see her again, to watch her face, to look into her grey-green eyes and hear her voice telling him stories of the horses she loved.

He remembered the little sob she had given when she related the suffering of Scham, and the compassion in her voice.

That was how a woman should be, he thought, compassionate towards pain, hurt and distressed by cruelty, and having an understanding of suffering which was unusual where sophisticated ladies of the social world were concerned.

Now that he had lost her the Earl felt himself being confronted by her qualities in an almost accusing manner.

How could he have been so blinded by his own importance as not to realize she was different from anyone else he had ever met?

All his life he had consciously and sometimes unconsciously looked for a woman who would take the place of his mother.

A woman who could offer him not only the attraction of physical desire but also something far more subtle, something spiritual, something for which he had instinctively reached out his arms but thought never to grasp.

Calista had been with him alone while he was recovering from his injuries, but he had not realized that she was everything he wanted and desired in a woman until he had lost her.

"Fool! Fool!" the Earl berated himself and knew he had no defence and no excuse for being so blind.

Without his being consciously aware of it his feet had carried him to the bridge over the Serpentine where he had waited for Calista that May morning which now seemed so long ago.

He remembered how Orestes had fidgeted and how because she was not there waiting for him his impulse had been to ride away.

Perhaps it would have been better if he had done so: then none of this long chain of disaster and anxiety would have happened!

And yet while his love for Calista humbled him because he had been so stupid and block-headed about it, he yet felt a pride and an elation because he loved and because she was so wonderful.

He supposed it was because he had suffered so much pain after his fight with Manzani that he had not, when he lay in the bed in the Inn, thought of her as a desirable woman, but only as someone who was kind and understanding, who waited on him, amused him and told him stories which made him forget his discomfort.

He had not realized at the time that it was extraordinary that he had not been bored, or even anxious to return to London to the comfort of his own home.

He had been content, but he had not realized it, any more than he had been aware that his contentment was entirely due to Calista.

It was only as the days passed that he

had found himself growing impatient when she was too long away from him because she was riding either Centaur or Orestes.

But still he had not understood why he watched the clock and felt his spirits rise when she came into the room in her green habit, her cheeks flushed from the exercise, the small tendrils of her red-gold hair which had been blown by the wind against her white forehead.

Always she seemed to bring the sunshine with her.

"What do you think happened this morning?" she would say with a little lilt in her voice.

Then he would find that his irritation had gone and he wanted to listen to what she had to say. Because she described the ride so vividly the Earl felt that he himself had been riding with her.

And still he had not understood why he felt that way!

The Earl reached the bridge over the Serpentine.

There were few people about because the crowds were clustered around the balloon waiting for the start of its ascent into the sky.

Here there was only peace and the shimmer of the water. The music of the Bands and the noise of the Fair was far away in the distance.

It was then that the Earl saw her—saw Calista!

She was standing at the very edge of the water and there was something in her attitude which made him draw in his breath.

She was bare-headed and wearing one of the plain muslin gowns that he knew so well.

She stood in the shadow of the bridge, her hair gleaming brightly against the grey stone and her body looking very slim and fragile.

As he watched her the Earl saw her bend a little further towards the water and with a sudden fear which struck through him like a knife he knew what she was about to do.

"Calista!" he ejaculated and his voice rang out.

She started and turned her head to look at him. He saw her face was very pale, her eyes seeming to fill it completely.

She stared at him as he advanced towards her.

"Calista!" he said again and now there was an appeal in his tone.

He had reached the top of the bank below which she stood, when with a cry she ran along the side of the water, climbed onto the grass and started to run wildly towards the crowd round the balloon.

"Calista — stop! Stop! the Earl shouted.

Then seeing that she did not intend to obey him he ran after her.

She was already some way ahead of him because he had been so surprised by her action, and he was also hampered by his tall hat and the cane he held in his hand.

Nevertheless he ran swiftly.

She sped on and now she started weaving her way through the crowd of spectators.

She pushed through them and only as she reached the men holding the ropes which kept the balloon down did she stop and look back over her shoulder.

The Earl was still some twenty yards behind her.

"Calista!" he called again. "Stop! Wait for me!"

Even above the noise of the crowd she must have heard him.

But she turned away and ran forward almost as if she was blind in her efforts to escape and was only arrested in her flight when she actually touched the car of the balloon.

She held on to it with both hands, then the Earl fighting his way through the crowd to get to her thought that her body seemed to sag as if she was exhausted.

Then even as he pushed through the last line of spectators he realized that the mooring ropes had been released and the balloon was ascending.

It was rising quickly, so quickly that Calista had not realized what was happening until she had been lifted off the ground.

The Earl rushed forward and the crowd, realizing what was happening, began to shout:

"Let go!" "Drop!" "You'll be carried away!"

But Calista still clung to the side of the red-painted car. She was now thirty or forty feet above the heads of the crowd, her skirts blowing in the breeze, her feet dangling like those of a doll.

Then as the Earl held his breath, incapable of crying out, and even the crowd was silent, a man's head and shoulders appeared above Calista and two hands clasped her wrists.

There was still a danger that she might fall until another man appeared and now they were lifting her, drawing her upwards and over the side of the car and into it.

A great shout went up from the crowd.

It was a cry of relief after the suspense they had suffered in fearing Calista must crash to the ground.

The balloon was above the tree-tops and rising still very fast upwards into the clear sky.

The Earl stood watching, with his head back, knowing helplessly there was nothing he could do, and feeling as if his brain had ceased to function.

He could think of nothing save that Calista was being taken away from him, almost as if she were disappearing from the world itself.

"Well — that's one way to get a cheap

flight!" he heard a man laugh.

"She'll find it cold in an hour or two," another answered. "I heard them say they didn't expect to be in France for at least sixteen hours!"

The Earl took one last look at the sky.

Now the balloon was only a small spot in the distance and the crowds were drifting away intent on finding other amusements.

He walked to the platform where Lord Palmerston was waiting for him.

"There you are, Helstone!" he exclaimed.

The Earl realized that from that side of the balloon no-one could have seen what had happened.

"I expect you want to get home," Lord Palmerston went on. "I know I shall be late for my dinner-party."

Lord Palmerston's carriage was waiting and they set off for Berkeley Square.

"Do you think Charles Green will reach Paris in safety?" the Earl asked.

He wondered if Lord Palmerston would notice that he was unable to speak naturally and that there was a strange note of anxiety in his voice.

"I am sure he will," Lord Palmerston replied. "He is very experienced and has made hundreds of successful ascents since I last saw him leave Vauxhall Gardens. I wonder if he will ever be able to cross the Atlantic?"

The Earl did not reply.

He was thinking of Calista being desperately cold as the balloon reached the great height that Charles Green expected of it.

Would they have extra clothing for themselves on board? he wondered.

He was sure that she was thinner than when he had last seen her, and if she was hungry as Centaur had been she would have less resistance to the cold.

Why had she run away from him like that? Why had she looked at him with a strange expression in her eyes that he could not understand?

The carriage came to a standstill.

"Thank you for accompanying me, Helstone," Lord Palmerston said. "Shall I see you tomorrow?"

"It is unlikely," the Earl replied. "I am going to France."

He stepped out of the carriage before

Lord Palmerston could question him further and hurried into his house.

He gave his orders sharply and concisely to the Butler, then ran upstairs to change his clothes and tell Travis he had exactly five minutes in which to pack what was required for a journey.

It said a great deal for the efficient organization of the Earl's household that little more than fifteen minutes later he was driving his Phaeton away from the doors of Helstone House and through the traffic towards the Dover Road.

The Prince Regent's record of reaching Brighton in two hours and fifty-three minutes had been broken many times since his death, but the Earl, although he did not trouble to check it, undoubtedly reached Dover in an all-time record.

Like many of his rich contemporaries he kept his own horses stabled on all the main roads, so that he was not obliged to drive the very inferior animals that were for hire at the Posting Inns.

On the Dover and Newmarket roads the Earl had some outstandingly fast horseflesh, so he was able to change his team frequently, taking no rest himself at any of the stopping places.

He did however drink a glass of wine at his last two stops and was, his valet noticed, completely unfatigued when they reached Dover before ten o'clock.

The Earl's yacht was kept in the harbour and was always, on his instructions, ready to sail at a moment's notice.

He sometimes had an urgent desire to get away from the social whirl and several times a year he would drive to Dover to go aboard *The Sea Horse*, to sail down the coast and return to the social scene as quickly and unexpectedly as he had departed.

Within twenty minutes of the Earl's coming aboard with Travis and his luggage the sails were run up and *The Sea Horse* was moving out of the harbour on the night breeze.

It was a moonlit night. The Earl stood for a long time on deck knowing they would have both a smooth crossing and a quick one, and was glad that his yacht was one of the fastest private vessels in commission.

He was determined, if possible to reach Calista as soon as she landed in France.

He knew where Charles Green was expecting to land, but that was not to say that change of wind or mistakes in navigation might not upset his plan.

He could not help remembering that the first time *The Royal Vauxhall* had set off to cross the Channel Charles Green had been intending to land in France, but had in fact ended up in Germany.

The balloon had stayed in the air for seventeen hours and Green had admitted the cold had been intense.

Although that was two years ago, since when Green had become much more experienced. The Earl found himself worrying in a manner which made him clench and reclench his hands at the thought of Calista shivering at some great altitude.

He did not realize even at this point how unusual it was for him to worry about anyone except himself.

He had never been beset by a moment's anxiety over the other beautiful women with whom he had spent so much of his time and on whom he had expended so much energy and expense.

What they did when they were not with him had never troubled his mind.

But now the only thing that mattered was that Calista should not suffer and that he could look after her and protect her as soon as she came down to earth.

Why? Why had she run away from him? He could find no answer to the question which challenged him over and over again in his mind.

Could she really dislike him to the point where she would scramble aboard a balloon rather than endure his presence?

Why had she contemplated, as he was sure she had, drowning herself in the Serpentine?

He had a feeling, although he did not know why, that she could not swim, and if she had in fact thrown herself into the water it was doubtful if anyone would have noticed her doing so.

It had been a perfect moment in which to be anonymous. Everybody was intent on the ascent of the balloon, and even if she had cried out involuntarily, no-one would have heard her.

But why? Why?

The question presented itself over and over again until the Earl felt he must go mad with the sheer repetition of it.

The road from Calais was rough going for the first few miles, and the only horses the Earl was able to hire were of inferior quality.

Had there been more time he would have taken his own Phaeton and the team with which he had entered Dover aboard with him, but he knew that the transport of horses by sea was always a difficult process which could not be hurried.

He therefore on disembarking at Calais instructed the Captain of *The Sea Horse* to return to Dover and pick up his Phaeton, his horses and grooms that would now be ready to embark and bring them across the Channel to Calais.

Although they had no looks and less breeding, the Earl managed to extract a considerable speed out of the French horses, for they were in fact well broken-in and easy to drive.

At the next Posting Inn the Earl had to admit to himself that the horses he obtained there were the equal of, if not better than, those available in similar establishments in England.

It was however late in the day when finally he drew near to Paris and had

300

some difficulty in finding the open ground where Charles Green had said he intended to land.

The Earl drove around some narrow lanes, enquired of several extremely slow-witted peasants whether they had seen a balloon, and finally when he was becoming frustrated and irritable Travis gave a cry and pointed with his finger.

"There, M'Lord! I can see it!"

The Earl peered between some tree-trunks and saw half collapsed on the ground, and looking in its deflated condition somewhat raffish in appearance, Charles Green's red and white striped balloon.

There were quite a number of people standing around it, and it was not difficult for the Earl to learn that the Aeronauts had repaired to the nearest Inn, the *Hôtellerie des Cloches* which, he was informed, was only a mile down the road.

His tired horses made a further effort and they were sweating as the Earl drew them to a standstill opposite a small but attractive Inn, such as could often be found on the outskirts of Paris.

Throwing his reins to Travis the Earl

climbed down from the barouche and walked into the Hostelry.

The *Patronne*, dressed in black, came forward to greet him and he asked abruptly in excellent French:

"Are the Aeronauts here, *Madame*, and is there a lady with them?"

"The Aeronauts are in the *Salle à manger, Monsieur*," the woman replied opened a door into a long low room set with tables where at one end, the Earl could see Charles Green.

He walked forward and the Aeronaut rose with an expression of astonishment.

"Is it possible that you have got here so quickly, My Lord?" he enquired.

"I have good reason for following you," the Earl replied. "My fiancée, Miss Chevington, was carried away with you by mistake!"

"Your fiancée?" Charles Green said in surprise, and added quickly:

"I can only say, My Lord, that it was very regrettable that the young lady should have been lifted off the ground when the balloon ascended, but as I hope you are well aware, there was nothing we could do but take her with us."

"She is all right?" the Earl asked.

Charles Green hesitated for a moment.

"She suffered intensely from the cold, My Lord. We arrived here half an hour ago, and she was taken straight upstairs and put to bed. I believe *Madame* has sent for a Doctor."

The Earl turned on his heel and left the *Salle à manger.*

The *Patronne* was waiting for him in the small hall.

"Will you please take me to the young lady who is ill?" he asked.

"Come this way, *Monsieur*."

He followed her upstairs.

The Hostelry was very old and the Earl guessed there were at the outside not more than two or three bedrooms to be let.

The *Patronne* opened a door.

Inside a small, low-ceilinged room the Earl could see Calista lying on a square French bed raised high with feather mattresses.

Beside her stood a man in a frock coat who he guessed was the Doctor, and there was also an elderly maid wearing a mob-cap and white apron in attendance.

The Doctor, who was taking Calista's pulse, did not look up as the Earl entered.

"Is that you, Madame Beauvais?" he said. "I want to talk to you about this young woman. She needs careful nursing."

"And that is what I wish you to arrange, *Monsieur*," the Earl replied.

The Doctor raised his head.

"Is she your wife, *Monsieur*?" he asked.

"No, *Monsieur*—my fiancée."

"Then you should take better care of her," the Doctor said sharply. "From all I hear of the manner in which she travelled here, the young lady will be extremely lucky if she escapes pneumonia!"

8

Calista moved restlessly and gave a little moan.

The Earl arose immediately from the armchair in which he had been sitting on the other side of the room and went to the bedside.

He could see she was still unconscious and her face was flushed. When he bent forward to touch her forehead tentatively with his fingers he knew she was running a high temperature.

The Doctor had told him what to expect.

"How long will she be unconscious, *Monsieur*?" the Earl had asked.

"I have no idea, Milord," the Doctor replied. "I am hoping that she will not develop pneumonia, but it is certain that she will run a fever."

"I would like an experienced nurse or nurses," the Earl said.

The Doctor looked doubtful.

"It would be impossible to find one tonight," he replied, "but tomorrow, Milord, I will bring you a Nun who is more experienced than anyone else I can supply."

"I can manage alone tonight," the Earl said.

"That will be a great help," the Doctor answered.

He gave the Earl instructions as to what medicines to administer if Calista should regain consciousness. Then after taking her pulse again he said:

"*Mademoiselle* is young and I imagine strong. The effects of such an experience should not be disastrous."

"We can only hope you are right, *Monsieur*," the Earl said.

"As always, Milord, it is in the lap of the gods," the Doctor replied cheerfully.

Travis had begged the Earl to let him sit up with Calista.

"You need your rest, M'Lord," he said. "You had a hard day yesterday and very little sleep last night while we were crossing the Channel."

"I had enough," the Earl replied, "and I prefer to look after Miss Chevington myself."

"You have only to ring the bell, M'Lord, and I will come to you immediately."

"I am sure of that," the Earl replied, "and thank you, Travis."

The Valet helped him undress and then wearing a long robe, the magnificence of which seemed out of place in the simple Hostelry, the Earl went into Calista's bedroom and checked to see if he had everything she might require in the night.

The Doctor's medicines looked unpalatable, but he hoped they would be effective.

There was freshly made lemonade in case she should be thirsty, and at the Earl's insistence some nourishing soup had been placed in a haybasket to keep it warm.

He had not forgotten that Centaur had been hungry when Calista had sent the horse to his stables, and he was certain that she would have spent her last penny before being ready to drown herself in the Serpentine.

The soup, *Madame* had informed him, was more nourishing than half a dozen beef-steaks and when it was taken from the hob in the kitchen and placed in the haybasket it was boiling hot. The Earl was sure it would be many hours before it cooled down.

Calista moaned again and moved her head from one side of the pillow to the other.

She also tried to throw off the bed-clothes; but the Earl pulled them over her again, knowing that it was essential to keep her warm.

It was in fact hot in the low-ceilinged bedroom and the night was warm outside.

After the Doctor left, the Earl had talked with Charles Green and learnt that at the high altitude the balloon had reached it had been exceedingly cold when darkness fell.

Charles Green and the two men who had accompanied him on the flight had wrapped Calista in the rugs they had taken with them, and one of them had actually taken off his fur-lined helmet and given it to her to wear.

The Earl expressed his gratitude; but he was well aware that the Aeronauts had found Calista a tiresome encumbrance, even though Charles Green was in fact used to women travelling in his balloon.

His wife was herself a very experienced Aeronaut and usually accompanied him on his flights.

The men were however anxious to reach Paris, in order to present Lord Palmerston's letter to the Foreign Secretary and also to give the newspapers the particulars and sketches of the Coronation they had carried with them.

Before they had finished their meal in the Hostelry some Officials had arrived to welcome Mr. Green. They told him that Paris was acclaiming another achievement in the air and that the Prime Minister was ready to receive him.

They therefore hurried away without showing much concern for Calista, and the Earl knew they were glad to be rid of the responsibility. He could not help wondering how she would have fared if he had not arrived.

His air of distinction and the fact that he was obviously a wealthy man made the *Patron* of the Hostelry and his wife only too anxious to do all in their power to provide everything he ordered.

It was not only Travis who offered to sit up with Calista; the chamber-maid proffered her services and so did *Madame* herself. But the Earl was determined that Calista should be his own responsibility.

Looking down at her as she moved restlessly, he thought how fragile she was.

Once again he was aware of that protective urge which he had never known in his life before. He wanted to save her not only from physical suffering but from unhappiness. He wanted to stand between her and the world and he knew with an undeniable certainty that he would never be happy unless she became his wife.

Her fair hair had fallen over her eyes and gently he pushed it back from her forehead, sitting down on the side of the bed as he did so.

"I am . . c . cold," she muttered, "so . . cold and I am . . falling . . I am . . afraid of . . falling."

"You are quite safe," the Earl said in his deep voice. "You are not cold, Calista, and there is no longer any possibility of your falling. You are safe."

She turned almost violently to the other side of the pillow and in quite a strong voice she cried out:

"Stop thief! . . Help! . . Stop him . . oh . . stop him!"

The Earl knew he had been right in guessing that someone must have robbed her and said quietly and calmly: "Go to sleep, Calista. There is no need to worry. You are safe and it is over."

"Centaur . . Centaur . . what are we to do?"

Now Calista's voice was very low and there was a frightened note in it which the Earl did not miss.

"You are hungry . . Oh, my dear . . I cannot bear you to be hungry . . and I am hungry too . . but we have no money . . nothing!" There was a pause and then she went on:

"I . . love . . him! I love him . . Centaur but I cannot tell him so . . he does not want to be tied . . he wants to be free . . he must . . never know . . never . . that I . . love him."

There was such poignancy in her voice that the Earl bent forward to put his arms around her.

With a convulsive gesture she turned and clung to him, her hand clasping the revers of his brocade robe.

"Help me . . Centaur," she whispered. "I am so unhappy . . so desperately . . miserable without him! But there is nothing we can do about it . . except go away. If he knew of my . . love for him he would be . . embarrassed and that I could not . . bear."

The Earl's arms tightened around her and she went on in a heartbreaking tone:

"He . . must . . never know. It must be a . . secret. He was right . . absolutely right Centaur . . we cannot . . manage on our own. You are hungry and I am hungry . . If I send you to him . . he will look after . . you."

She gave a little sigh and then in a voice that seemed to pierce the Earl in his very heart she murmured:

"Without . . you and without . . him, Centaur . . there is . . nothing I can do but . . die . . die."

The Earl held her very close.

"You are not going to die," he said gently. "You are going to live. Go to sleep, Calista. I promise you that everything will be all right."

As if his words reached through to her,

she cuddled closer to him.

"I . . love . . him! I . . love . . him with
all . . my . . heart."

.   .   .

The Nun came into the bedroom carrying a huge vase of lilies.

Calista sat up in bed and gave a little
laugh of delight.

"How lovely! I have always been fond
of lilies."

"And so have I," the Nun replied.
"They are the flowers of the Mother of
God and have a special sanctity about
them."

"I love their fragrance," Calista said.

"I will stand them near your bed," the
Nun smiled and she put the vase down on
a table near Calista.

She was a sweet-faced woman of over
forty, wearing the robes of the Poor Sisters
of Mary who spent their time tending to
the sick and to the aged.

In the week since she had recovered
consciousness Calista had grown to have a
very real affection for the woman who
owned no possessions but dedicated

herself to the service of others.

"Has His Lordship returned?" Calista asked now.

"He came back from Paris about a quarter of an hour ago," the Nun replied. "He had a gentleman with him and they are at the moment having dinner downstairs."

"I ate everything that was brought me tonight," Calista said. "I shall grow fat if I stay here much longer. The food is so delicious."

The Nun smiled.

"And you are well, *ma petite*. The Doctor has said you can get up tomorrow, but you must be very careful with yourself."

"I feel quite well," Calista said, "and all I want is to be out in the sunshine. I am tired of being in bed."

The Nun laughed.

"Yes, indeed, you are well again and so you will have no further need of my services."

Calista looked at her apprehensively.

"You are not leaving me?"

"I shall not be coming here tomorrow," the Nun replied. "There are other people who are sick, who need my attention, and as you say yourself you are now well."

"But I do not wish to lose you," Calista cried. "You have been so kind, so very kind to me!"

"I have been happy looking after you," the Nun replied, "but in our Order we try not to grow too attached to our patients. If we do, it is always painful to leave them."

"I hate to say good-bye," Calista said wistfully.

"Milord will look after you. He is very devoted and he was extremely anxious when you were so ill."

Calista did not answer but looked down, her eyelashes dark against her pale cheeks.

It was true, as the Nun had said, that the Earl had shown himself extremely attentive all through her illness in the Hostelry.

Their roles had been reversed: now it was the Earl who sat by her bed-side to tell her stories of what was happening outside, who played chess with her and brought her books to read.

She had at first been too weak even to

talk with him. Then with the elasticity of youth she had grown stronger every day and the delicious nourishing food seemed to give her new strength after each meal.

The Earl, however, had not questioned her about what had happened, but she knew that sooner or later they must talk together about it.

She would have to try to offer an explanation for running away from him when he had found her at the Serpentine, and why she had been so foolish as to be carried away by the balloon.

Even to think of that terrifying experience made Calista tremble.

It had at first been fascinating as they ascended quickly into the sky to see the world below growing smaller and smaller and the people including the Earl vanishing from sight.

Then as they still climbed, she became acutely conscious that she was wearing only a thin muslin dress and had not even a bonnet to cover her hair.

Charles Green of course had scolded her for clinging to the side of the car.

"How could you do anything so stupid, so ridiculous, as to be swept away in such a manner?" he stormed.

"I remember some years ago there was a boy who did just the same thing," one of the Aeronauts remarked.

"That was different!" Charles Green snapped. "He was caught in the mooring-ropes and had to be hauled aboard because there was nothing else they could do about him."

"And there is nothing else we can do about this stowaway," the man remarked with a smile.

That was true, Calista realized. They could hardly drop her overboard, and when her teeth began to chatter and she was shivering, Charles Green's anger evaporated and he provided her with all the wraps there were available.

Nevertheless she grew colder and colder in the darkness of the night.

Later when the balloon was deflated in order to descend it was more frightening than anything she had imagined. She thought she must fall into a tree or be deposited in a lake.

She was utterly terrified.

She knew she had no-one to blame but herself; but to see the Earl standing just above her on the bank of the Serpentine at the very moment that she had decided to plunge into the water beneath the bridge, had been such a shock that she had no time to think.

Her only thought was that she must escape from him; that he must not realize the plight she was in, or the reason why she had run away from him in the first place.

She knew only too well what he felt about their intended marriage. He was putting a good face on it, but he had no wish to be married.

He wanted to be free, and she could not face the sort of marriage he had suggested to her.

Loving him as she did, how could she endure his idea that they could build a marriage on "interests in common", and what he had called an "intelligent determination" to make each other happy.

"I love him! I love him!" she told herself and knew that it would be impossible to live if he was kind to her merely out of pity or of necessity.

"I want his love," she whispered and thought there could be no agony so intense as loving a man who could not reciprocate.

The Nun came back into the bedroom wearing her black cloak in which she would return to the Convent.

"*Au revoir, ma petite*. It has been a great pleasure to know you, and may God bring you much happiness in the future."

"Thank you," Calista replied, thinking that was unlikely, "and thank you, dear Sister Teresa, for looking after me and for making me well again."

She would have liked to kiss the Nun, but she felt that might be inappropriate. So instead they shook hands, and there was a suspicion of tears in Calista's eyes as Sister Teresa left the bedroom.

'Now, I shall be alone with the Earl,' Calista thought and wondered what his plans were, now she was well enough to leave the Hostelry.

She heard his footsteps coming up the staircase and nervously twisted her fingers together.

Sister Teresa had already tidied her hair before dinner, and she was wearing one of the beautifully embroidered silk nightgowns which the Earl had bought for her in Paris and a soft silk shawl trimmed with wide lace.

As well as the lilies, the room was full of other flowers.

Every day the Earl had brought her roses and carnations of every colour, which he had bought in the flower market in Paris or from the flower-women who proffered their wares on the steps of the Madeleine.

The room, Calista thought, looked more like a bower than a bedroom, and she hoped as she waited for the Earl that he would think she looked attractive.

There was now more colour in her face, and she was not as thin as she had been when she had first felt well enough to look at herself in the mirror.

The door opened and the Earl came in.

She was immediately aware how elegant he looked in his evening clothes and how tall and broad-shouldered he appeared in the low room.

Then with a surprise she realized he was not alone! following behind him was another man.

The Earl advanced towards the bed and Calista saw he had a bouquet of flowers in his hands, all white. There were white carnations, roses and lilies of the valley.

She looked at them and then at the man who had entered behind the Earl and saw he was wearing a surplice.

Her eyes were frightened as she looked up at the Earl standing beside her bed.

"Canon Barlow, of the British Embassy Church in Paris, Calista," he said quietly, "has kindly come here to marry us."

As Calista gave a little gasp, the Earl put the bouquet down in front of her and took her hand in his.

He knew that she was trembling and he said gently:

"It will not be a long service."

Calista wanted to speak but somehow her voice had died in her throat.

She could only look at the Earl with frightened eyes and then, as he smiled at her reassuringly, the Canon, opening his prayer-book, began the service of marriage.

The Earl made his responses in a firm, strong voice while Calista's in contrast was very low, hardly above a whisper.

Yet the beautiful words were said, and when the ring was on her finger and their hands were joined together, the Canon blessed them.

There was a silence as his voice died away. Then closing the prayer-book he said in an ordinary tone:

"May I be the first to congratulate you, My Lord? And Lady Helstone; may I wish you every happiness now and for ever?"

"Thank you," Calista managed to murmur.

"I know you are in a hurry to return to Paris, Canon," the Earl remarked. "My carriage is waiting outside for you."

"Thank you," the Canon replied. "I have a rather important appointment at nine o'clock."

"You will be in time for it."

"I am sure I shall. Your horses, My Lord, are outstanding."

"I am glad you think so," the Earl said politely. The two men left the room and Calista could hear their footsteps receding down the uncarpeted wooden staircase.

She sat still, but her head was in a whirl!

How could this have happened? Why had the Earl married her with such haste and without warning her of his intention?

She had been considering a number of arguments to persuade him that he need not commit himself into becoming her husband unwillingly; but she had felt there was plenty of time for them to talk things over and argue it out.

Yet now this had happened!

She wondered why she had not immediately protested when he brought the Clergyman into the room, but she knew she had been too surprised, in fact utterly bewildered, to do anything except obey his directions!

She was his wife!

And even as an irrepressible thrill arose in her at the thought, she heard him coming back up the stairs.

He came into the room and closing the door behind him he stood looking at her — at her fair hair with the touches of red framing the frightened little white face with a question in her grey-green eyes.

He smiled and she thought he looked happy.

"It is hot tonight," he said in an ordinary tone of voice. "Will you forgive me if I take off my coat?"

Without waiting for her reply, he pulled

off his smart and close-fitting coat and threw it down on a chair.

In his thin muslin shirt, with his exquisitely tied cravat, he looked at ease and very masculine.

Calista was unable to meet his eyes, and the colour rose in her cheeks as he crossed the room and sat down on the bed to face her.

He did not speak and after a moment she said in a whisper:

"Why . . did you . . marry me like . . that?"

"There are three good reasons," he answered. "First because I felt it only fair to Centaur that we should legalize his position. He told me he was fed up with being pushed from pillar to post."

Calista gave a faint smile as if she could not help it.

"Secondly," the Earl continued, "I am really too old to be continually beaten up in Circuses and forced to swim the Channel to catch up with a balloon!"

Calista gave a little choke of laughter and the Earl went on:

"And lastly, although this is far the most important, I love you, my darling."

She was very still. Then as her eyes sought his he said gently:

"It is true! I love you. I cannot live without you — nor do I intend to risk losing you again."

"Are . . you . . sure?"

"I am very sure," he replied. "I did not know it was possible to suffer such agony as you have inflicted on me since you disappeared from the Inn. How could you do anything so cruel?"

Her eyes fell before his, and as he put his hand over hers he knew she was trembling.

"I thought you wanted to be . . free and I could not bear to be married to someone who did not want . . me."

"Even though it was someone you loved?" the Earl asked.

She looked up at him quickly and the colour rose in her face.

"How did you know . . that?"

"You told me so."

"Do you mean . . when I was unconscious?"

"You told me all the things that I wanted to hear," he answered. "That you loved me and that you were prepared to die because of that love."

Calista gave a little murmur of embarrassment and instinctively she moved towards him so that she could hide her face against his shoulder.

He held her very close.

"I was such a fool," he said. "I did not realize that you were what I have been looking for all my life — a woman who would love me for myself and who would care for me so much that her love was utterly and completely selfless."

His arms tightened as he went on:

"At the same time, my precious one, how dare you try to destroy yourself when you are mine and you belong to me?"

"I could not bear you to be . . kind to me only because you . . pitied me," Calista said.

"I should have told you that I loved you when we were at the Inn together. But I was such a blockhead I did not realize that the emotions you awoke in me and which I had never felt before were what I had always been seeking."

He gave a little laugh as he said:

"I was so crazily, wildly jealous of the Clown who had laid his heart at your feet!

I was jealous of the horses who absorbed so much of your attention! But even then I did not understand it was love, not until I had lost you and thought I should never find you."

"You really . . minded?" Calista whispered.

"You will never leave me again," the Earl said firmly. "I could not bear it, I could not live again through all the pain and anxiety of these last few weeks."

He pulled her a little closer as he said:

"You have a lot to answer for, my sweet, but I have grown wiser through bitter experience. That is why I married you tonight. I had no intention of letting you leave this bedroom until you were actually my wife."

"You love me? You really . . love me?" Calista asked as if she could not believe it was true.

"I shall have to prove it," the Earl said, "so that you will no longer be in any doubt. There is plenty of time ahead of us for me to do that."

He bent his head as he spoke and at the same time put his fingers under Calista's chin and turned her face up to his. Then his mouth was on hers.

She felt a sensation such as she had never known before seep through her body and rise like a warm wave up to her throat and into her lips.

It was so glorious, so perfect that she knew this was love. This was what she had wanted to find in the man she married, and for him to find in her.

It was a wonder, a glory, a rapture, such as she had never dreamt existed in the world.

Then as the Earl felt her lips respond to him and the softness of her body seemed to melt against him, his kiss grew more demanding, more passionate, more insistent.

Calista felt the room whirl around and disappear so that she and the Earl were alone in the sunlight and there was nothing else but their love.

The Earl raised his head.

"I love you, my elusive darling, I love you. I did not know that any woman could be so beautiful, so perfect and so sweet."

"I love . . you," Calista whispered. "This is how I . . always knew . . love would be if I could only . . find it."

"We have found it together," the Earl said and he kissed her eyes, her cheeks, her small nose, and then again her lips.

A long time passed before Calista said hesitatingly:

"Shall we have to go back at . . once to tell Mama and the other people we are . . married?"

"We are not going back until we have had a long honeymoon."

The Earl saw the light that lit Calista's eyes.

"We can be . . alone?"

"Quite alone," he replied with a smile, "unless you count the horses I have bought for you."

"Horses!" Calista questioned.

"I think they will meet with your approval. They have the Arab strain in them."

"Oh, how wonderful!" Calista cried. "I have so often dreamt of riding with you. It is what I have wanted to do above all else."

The Earl kissed her gently and then he said:

"I have made a lot of plans. First we

will go to Paris because, although I have bought you a few dresses, my precious, I have a feeling that you will require quite an extensive trousseau and who could provide that better than the couturiers of Paris?"

"All I want is a riding-habit!" Calista said impulsively. "No, that is not true! I want to look pretty for . . you."

"You look lovely in anything you wear," the Earl said, "even in those disreputable pantaloons and that jockey's jacket in which you appeared the night we walked in the garden together!"

"I shocked you?" Calista smiled.

"I am still shocked!" he replied. "I promise you I shall not allow you to wear them again except when we are absolutely alone together."

Calista laughed.

"In which case," she said, "I might as well wear what I am wearing now . . which is practically . . nothing!"

The Earl smiled but there was a hint of fire in his eyes.

"I said then you were a provocative little devil! Are you trying to provoke me, my darling?"

She blushed at the passion in his voice and hid her face against his shoulder.

"When we are bored with Paris," the Earl said more gently, "I think we might go on to Vienna. I know it would make you happy to see the Lipizzan stallions in the Spanish Riding School."

She gave a little cry of sheer delight.

"How could you think of anything so marvellous? It is something I would love to do more than anything else in the world!"

Then shyly she added:

"But it will only be . . wonderful because . . you are with me."

"You will be able to learn some new tricks to teach Centaur, and when we get home we can start trying to breed a new Eclipse."

The Earl paused then added very softly:

"And perhaps we can try together to produce an exceptional progeny of our own."

"I know that any son of . . yours," Calista whispered, "would be as . . magnificent as Godolphin Arabian."

"And any daughter of yours, my lovely one," the Earl replied, "would be as beautiful as Rozana."

She clung to him and the Earl felt her quiver as she trembled at his touch.

"I have a present for you," he said as he kissed her hair.

He bent forward to pull his discarded coat towards him and take from the pocket a thin, paper-covered book. When Calista saw it she exclaimed with delight:

"It is the book that Coco had! The book that contains the stories about Scham and Agba!"

"I found it in an old bookshop," the Earl told her. "Now you will be able to read me the rest of the tales."

"Oh, thank you!"

"I have another present but I doubt if it is so exciting."

As he spoke he took from his other pocket a ring. It was a large circular diamond surrounded by smaller ones, and taking her left hand he put it on her third finger above the wedding ring that already encircled it.

"It is lovely . . quite lovely," Calista exclaimed and added anxiously, "it must have been very expensive."

"You could have had at least three

horses for the price of it," the Earl teased.

"Thank you! Thank you so much!" Calista said and lifted her lips to his.

He pulled her almost roughly against him. His kiss was passionate and there was a fire about it that awoke a flame within Calista.

She clung to him, feeling as if her whole body responded to what he demanded of her. She did not quite understand what that was, she only knew she wanted to be closer to him.

She wanted him to go on kissing her. She wanted the fire in his lips to consume her utterly until there was nothing of herself left and she was a part of him.

Then as abruptly as the Earl had embraced her he suddenly released her.

"You must not get over-tired," he said in a voice that was unsteady. "I must let you go to sleep, Calista, so that you will be rested for tomorrow when you come downstairs for the first time."

He rose to his feet as he spoke and she looked up at him.

Her lips were very soft and a little tremulous from the violence of his kisses and her eyes had a strange light in them.

"Are you . . leaving . . me?" she asked in a very small voice.

"I want you to go to sleep."

"But . . I thought . ." she stopped uncertainly.

The Earl was very still.

"What do you think?" he asked after a moment.

"That . . now we are . . married," she whispered, "you would . . stay with me."

He did not reply and after a moment she said hastily:

"But . . only if you . . want to."

"Want to!"

It was a cry which came from the very depth of the Earl's being. Then his arms were around her, holding her so tightly it was hard to breathe.

"I love you, I adore you, I worship you," he said fervently, "and you ask me if I want to stay! Oh, my precious darling! My little love! There are no words in which I can tell you how much I desperately and agonizingly want you!"

Then his lips were on hers holding her completely and utterly captive. She put her arms round his neck and felt her body move beneath his, their hearts beating against each others.

She was his, irrevocably his, as he was hers. They were no longer elusive, no longer two separate people, but one.

This was what she had dreamt of, longed for, and prayed that she might find. It was part of the Divine and all the beauty of the world.

"My sweet, my darling, my adorable wife," the Earl murmured hoarsely.

And Calista knew that all their lives they would gallop side by side down the straight, neck to neck, towards the winning post of Love!